"Designed by Fate"
A Lesbian Romance

Jenny Bloom

This book is intended for Adults (ages 18+) only. The contents may be offensive to some readers. It may contain graphic language, explicit sexual content, and adult situations. May contain scenes of unprotected sex. Please do not read this book if you are offended by content as mentioned above or if you are under the age of 18. Please educate yourself on safe sex practices before making potentially life-changing decisions about sex in real life.

This story is a work of fiction. Names, characters, businesses, places, events and incidents are the products of the author's imagination or used in a fictitious manner & are not to be construed as real. Any resemblance to actual persons, living or dead, or actual events is purely coincidental. Products or brand names mentioned are trademarks of their respective holders or companies. The cover uses licensed images & are shown for illustrative purposes only. Any person(s) that may be depicted on the cover are simply models.

Edition v1.00 (2020.04.27)
www.JennyBloomAuthor.com

Special thanks to the following volunteer readers who helped with proofreading: RB, JayBee, Naomi W., Jenny and those who assisted but wished to be anonymous. Thank you so much for your support.

Chapter One

Shelby Morgan had brought her portfolio in the hopes that this was what they wanted. She had her hands gripped against her black pants, and as her green eyes looked over at the other women who were standing near the doorway, she felt the onslaught of anxiety come over her as she looked at all of them.

They were all women hoping that the designers here would notice them. If the designers didn't care, they'd just go on their merry way, and go on creating more. Shelby was banking on it.

She remembered the email she got earlier that day while heading to the classroom for her first workshop on installing invisible zippers quickly. It was from her mom and dad.

Shelby,

We are watching your progress. Shouldn't you just give up? You've been at the school for almost four years, and you don't have an internship or anything. It's almost over so…what are you going to do then? We're not going to support you through everything Shelby; you'll have to learn to take life into your own hands. Look at your future. There is still time. You can go into a field that is useful to you, not just some frilly dresses and a waste of time.

Mom

Shelby deleted the email before she could even respond. She was that upset over what her mother said.

She didn't think it was fair. It wasn't fair that her mother thought of her like that. She just saw everything Shelby did as a waste of time. It truly wasn't fair.

All Shelby wanted was for people to take her seriously, even if it meant that it would be awkward at first. She didn't want to continue beating around the bush with this, she just wanted a normal life, with a normal job, and normal, supportive parents.

Instead, she got this.

Shelby waited as more and more women were called in. They would head inside, hear the woman on the other side tell them how bad they were, and how they needed to work on their designs. Then, there was always someone else inside who was the coldest of them all. This woman wouldn't say much more than "Get out." Shelby wondered if this person even regarded anyone as good here.

The woman was crotchety. Shelby didn't like the feeling the unknown woman gave her.

As more and more women came out disappointed by it all, Shelby began to realize the truth. She was potentially going to get the same treatment as these people.

All her hard work, all of the endeavors she got into, it made her wonder if there was someone out there who saw her for the potential that she had. After a little bit, she heard her name called.

"Shelby Morgan," the woman at the front of the doorway said.

Shelby looked around, hearing the whisperings from a few of the models.

"Oh look, it's the fourth year who still doesn't have an internship," one said.

"Isn't she graduating soon? Does she think she has a shell of a chance right now? Please, I can already see she's screwed," another woman said.

They both laughed, and Shelby could feel her ears burning, but she shook it off.

"I'll show you. I'll nail an internship here, even if it's the last thing I do," she said to herself.

She looked forward, and then opened the door. In there was a panel of judges, and Shelby felt their eyes on her green ones. Shelby wanted to run her hands through her brown pixie cut, since that was what she would do whenever she was nervous. She walked forward, her curvy body moving toward the table there.

"Hello," she said.

"Hello there," another voice said.

"You're Shelby Morgan, correct?" the other person next to them asked. He was a guy with a deep accent.

"Yes sir. Fourth year student," she said, her voice mousey. Shelby could feel their eyes widen in slight surprise at these words.

"Why don't you have an internship yet? Don't you know how important those are?" the lady that was directly across from Shelby asked. She had long, beautiful brown hair that cascaded like a river and piercing blue eyes that made her feel like they were staring directly into Shelby's soul.

Shelby was frightened.

For the first time, she felt utterly scared. She had no idea what would happen next, or even what to do, and it made her wonder if there was anything more she could do at this point. She felt like she already lost every goddamn chance at this the moment she walked in.

"No, you're not leaving yet," the brown-haired beauty said.

"Okay," she replied.

She sat there, looking at the three of them with tense eyes. She felt fear, and for the first time in a long time, she wanted nothing more than to hide in her childhood bedroom. The one across from her then grasped the portfolio, holding it forward and looking at it.

"Interesting. Any reason why you haven't gotten an internship yet?" she asked.

"No ma'am. I've never been given the opportunity. I really hope one of you will consider me. I've been a little desperate for an internship," she said.

The brown eyed woman stared at Shelby with a look that made her feel like she was trying to understand the true form of her. Shelby felt naked underneath that stare, but at the same time, it felt nice.

"I see. Well, your style could use some work. You are way too into those bright colors. Not everything needs some bright and flashy design," she snapped.

"Sorry," Shelby said.

"Come now, don't do that either. This is a critique, and if you can't handle it, then please, do leave right now," she said.

"I understand. I don't mind criticisms. I just feel like you hate me," Shelby said.

The woman laughed.

"You've got it all wrong, my dear," she said.

Wait, so she didn't hate her? What the hell was this lady getting at? Shelby felt her heart beat at the speed of light as the brown-haired lady began to speak.

"My name is Tasha Gambino. You've probably heard of me, either in a positive, or negative manner. Either way, I really don't care," Tasha explained.

"I see, Miss Tasha," Shelby stammered.

"Drop that *Miss* crap. It's just Tasha. Anyway, you are quite interesting. It's Shelby, correct? Do you have brothers and sisters?" she asked.

"A brother, but he's a lawyer in Chicago," Shelby said.

"Ah, big time Chicago boy then. I'm going to say that you have a good style. However, it's quite limited," Tasha said.

"I'm sorry ma'am," Shelby said, trying her best to keep herself together. The last thing she wanted was for Tasha to get mad, but then, Tasha sighed.

"I see. Well, I'll tell you something there Shelby, if you want to become a better fashion designer, you need to work on this. You need to start taking risks, and making changes," she said.

"I'll try to," Shelby said.

"Well, I think I know what my answer is. You're certainly shooting far lower than the other women around here. But, there's something different about you. Maybe it's because you actually know your worth, and your place?" Tasha said.

Was that supposed to be a compliment? Shelby wasn't sure. Over time, she could feel the tension growing as she sat there. As she looked at Tasha, Shelby tried to figure out what to do next.

"What do you suppose we do then? Should I just leave?" Shelby said.

"Of course not. We haven't made our verdict yet. I'm sure you know the answer though," Tasha snapped. The tone of her voice made Shelby wonder if she made the right decision even doing her portfolio for these people. Tasha seemed like a bitch. She wasn't concerned about the people she was looking at.

"Well, I don't want anything to do with that. It's an utter disaster," the man with the accent said.

"She's not the kind of woman I want under my internship. I'm sorry, but maybe you'll get lucky outside of school," the other lady said.

Shelby knew this was coming, but that didn't make it hurt any less. She stood there, preparing herself for the words that Tasha was about to utter, the rejection she could already hear coming.

"You're now under my wing. Get used to it."

Chapter Two

Tasha didn't understand why she wanted this woman so badly. What did Shelby have that immediately grabbed her?

It didn't make sense. Her work was slipshod at best, complete crap at worst. She tried her best to be nice, and she wondered if it was even possible to be skillful like that.

But, there was something about this which intrigued Tasha, which made her realize she wanted her on her team, even if it meant she was dealing with someone who was utterly worthless, and who didn't know a rat's ass from their face regarding fashion.

She didn't understand why she even said those words, but she did. It was something which surprised even her.

It was amazing that this was even the case; that she felt this way about it. She wondered if it was just fate playing some cruel trick on her as she uttered the words there.

But, when Shelby looked at her, her eyes wide as saucers, and her mouth agape, Tasha knew she'd done something; she just wasn't sure if it was a good thing or not.

"You're serious?"

"Does it look like I'm joking?" Tasha snapped.

She knew Shelby was naïve, but this was a whole new level. She wondered if this was the right choice.

The other two designers looked at Tasha with surprise on their faces.

"But Tasha, even you see she's a disaster,"

"Yes, Tasha. This isn't like you," Angela replied.

"I know, but I want to see what potential she has. There's something about her which...intrigues me. She'll be in for a rude awakening when she realizes this is far from easy of course, but I'm sure she'll like the thrill of it all," Tasha said with a haughty smile.

Tasha watched as Shelby blushed. Even though she didn't take Shelby seriously whatsoever, there was something about this which made her feel cool, like she was on top, like she had control.

Maybe that was it. That feeling of control that she couldn't get with anyone else.

"So, what now?" Shelby said.

"Well, I think you were the last one, so you're free to come with me. I'll have you finish the last of the paperwork, and then, I'll be seeing you for the internship starting Monday. You can come see me after classes and we'll have a nice little time together," Tasha purred.

Tasha could see that Shelby was feeling nervous and while she understood the sentiment, at the same time, she also felt like she didn't have to be so on edge.

"Relax, I'm not going to hurt you," she said.

Shelby looked around the room as the other man, and the woman walked off, both of them looking down at Shelby. Tasha just grimaced.

"Whatever; not like they have any room to talk. I've seen the boys Pierre has hired. A bunch of little bitches who probably are only there because he fucks them on the regular," Tasha said. She knew she wouldn't hear the end of this for a while, but there was something about her choice which made her wonder if she really did make the correct decision. Deep down, she honestly thought that she did.

"So, what do I need to do?" Shelby asked.

Tasha fiddled for the contract. She always brought one with her if she felt like there was potential there.

"Here it is. Read it over, sign it, and from there, we'll start you on your internship," Tasha explained.

She watched as Shelby read it over, but then, she stopped.

"This internship is paid."

"You seriously thought I'd just ask for you to come with me and not pay you? What kind of person do you think I am?" Tasha asked.

Shelby blushed, and for a moment, Tasha had to admit that Shelby was pretty cute as she did that. She liked the awkward, blushing types, but then, she spoke.

"I'm sorry. I'm just surprised. I didn't think you liked anyone, let alone me. You were berating me the entire time in front of them. I thought you'd be the first person to reject me. Not like I wouldn't be used to it or anything," Shelby said.

Seriously? This woman also had an inferiority complex and was cute? Wow, she really struck gold on this one.

"Of course not. Don't be stupid. You're a valuable investment. I can see the potential there," Tasha pointed out.

"Really now? But why?" Shelby asked.

Was it really that weird? Tasha didn't think it was, but then again, she also knew how people could be about this kind of thing. It made sense in its own way, kind of.

"Well Shelby, I can see how nervous you are, and how you're unsure about whether or not you should do this. Well, I'm here to tell you that I don't have any petty qualms with you or anything. I know that you suck. I acknowledge that. I'd have to be blind as a bat to not see that. And yet, there's something about you that makes me want to take a chance, that makes me want to see where this relationship goes," she said.

Tasha blushed as she uttered those words. Looking over at Shelby, she saw she had tears in her eyes. *Christ, she is one of those types too.*

"You are serious, right?" she asked.

"Does it look like I'm joking?" Tasha snapped.

Shelby then wiped the tears from her eyes. Tasha watched as Shelby sighed.

"No one has given me a chance. Maybe it's a pity motion, but I really do appreciate it," Shelby said.

"You're most welcome. But, please prove to me that I made a wise choice. I'm second guessing myself even as we speak," she said.

Tasha just wanted to see Shelby be thankful. There was something about her that was warming her cold heart. In a strange way, this was a new beginning for her.

This was the first person she trusted in a long time.

"Thank you, thank you so much. You seriously don't know how much this means to me. Will I be working with anyone else currently?" Shelby inquired.

Tasha tensed for a moment, gripping the desk and shaking her head.

"No, it's just you and me. Why, can't handle that?"

"Not at all. I was just curious, since well, I kind of expected you to have another assistant or something," Shelby said.

"There's a reason why I don't work with others, Shelby. For now, I'd rather not tell you the details behind that," Tasha said.

Shelby looked over at her, quickly nodding.

"I'm sorry if I intruded," she muttered.

"Don't worry about it. I know how it is. But I don't have any other partners, Shelby. You're my only intern. I hope it isn't a problem or anything," Tasha said.

Right now, she just hoped this would be okay. Tasha had never taken on an intern before. Perhaps, Shelby, who was utterly terrible at everything, could make it work.

"All right, I'll do it then. Give me the contract. I'll sign it," Shelby said.

Tasha whistled in surprise. "Are you sure, Shelby? I don't want you to feel pressured or anything," she asked.

"I think I'll be all right," Shelby said.

She wrote down the details on the sheet, singing and dotting everything. She then went with the final line, signing it and looking over at Tasha, and then, she spoke.

"All right, it's done. What else do I have to do today?" she asked.

"Absolutely nothing Shelby. You can head on out. It was a pleasure to meet you," she said.

"All right," she replied.

Shelby ran out and Tasha followed, after gathering the papers. The address was written on the contract, but Shelby did give her number so Tasha could text her where to meet. It would be at the school of course, for the first time, but as Tasha looked at the papers, she began to feel a heaviness in her heart.

Did she do the right thing? This was the first person ever to be added as an intern to her team.

"Why the hell did you do that?" a voice said.

Tasha looked over, noticing Angela there. It was one of her peers, and a rival designer. "I don't know honestly. I feel like it was right. In its own way," she said.

"You think it's right? Are you sure about that?" Angela asked.

"I'm not sure, but I did it anyway. I just wanted to see if it was the right thing," she said.

"I swear Tasha, you're going to drop her after the first day. I can already tell. Besides, we need to start working on the Spring and Summer Collections," Angela said.

"I know. I know it's a lot on my plate, but I want to take her on, have her by my side, and see what I can do to whip her into shape. You don't think it's a bad thing, right?" she asked.

"No, but I think you're the one who is making a foolish mistake there," she said.

As Angela walked off, Tasha looked at the piece of paper.

For the first time, Tasha didn't feel lonely when she was around someone. Why did Shelby make her feel this way? It was like she touched that cold heart of hers, and she wondered what to do about any of this.

"I don't get it, but I guess there's no room for me to question this either," she muttered to herself.

It was definitely not easy for her to understand, but at the same time, there was definitely potential in all of this. She wanted to see where this would go, and where the future would lead for all of them.

But what she didn't know was this would change her life and letting someone in would make a difference in the future.

Chapter Three

Shelby stood outside the door where the portfolio presentations happened, shaking in surprise. All of that work, all that time she put into it, and it was now culminating to something.

"But, how?" she asked herself, shaking her head as she tried to figure out how all of this happened.

She couldn't believe it. As Shelby went over to her study space, one of the other students from earlier that she spoke to occasionally came over. She had tears in her eyes, and a look of complete defeat on her face.

"I can't believe we had to do a portfolio presentation for them of all people. The last thing I wanted, to be quite honest," she said.

"Hey Danica. Did you get treated like utter crap too?" Shelby said.

"Yes. I expected that from Tasha. But, the other two? That really hurt," Danica said.

"I was a little shocked myself. I'm still shaking," Shelby said.

"You're not even that good at this sort of thing. I wonder what they said to you," Danica replied, looking at Shelby in a forlorn manner.

"Don't pity me, Danica. They offered me the job. Well, Tasha did," Shelby said.

"You're kidding," Danica said.

"No. I'm not. Why do you say that?" Shelby asked.

"Tasha doesn't just hire anyone," she said.

"I know that. I know she's never had an intern before, but she offered me the position, and I don't want to refuse it. I'm just a little bit surprised, that's all," Shelby said.

"You should be. You know that she's *never* taken an intern ever, right?" Danica pointed out.

"I guess she wants to try something new. I'm not complaining," Shelby said.

"You might as well be the moment she puts you through the ringer with everything she wants done. You know she's got a reputation for no-nonsense," she asked.

"Yes, but don't they all?" Shelby asked. She expected that to be the case.

"No. This woman used to be a model, so she's a big name. She's beautiful, and still looks incredibly young. She's been in the business for a long time," Danica said.

Shelby looked at her peer, and she realized what she was getting into. This wouldn't be your average little internship. This would put her through it all, and for a moment, she wondered if she made the right decision.

"I'm not backing out now," Shelby said.

"It's too late on that one," Danica pointed out.

"I thought she might offer me a chance to leave, but I doubt it. But, I'm willing to face the challenge. I want to prove to my parents I'm worth a damn. I feel like Tasha can help with that," Shelby said.

"Fine, but you might regret it," Danica pointed out.

Shelby sighed. She knew Danica was like that when it came to people who were out of her league. For some strange reason, Shelby wanted to see where this went.

"You need to relax, Danica. I'm sure everything will be okay," Shelby said.

"You're right. I'm worried it might be too much for you, and you'll get overwhelmed."

"No, I'm just glad to finally have something. To prove to my parents that I'll be successful," Shelby said.

She couldn't wait to gloat to her parents. She wanted to prove to them that she was stronger than this, and that she was better than this. After a little bit, Shelby got up, heading out and going to her apartment. She lived alone, but she preferred that. It was easier this way.

It gave Shelby more time to process what just happened, especially with her encounter with all those people.

She thought a lot about all of the aspects of the encounter that she experienced. She knew that this would either work in her favor, or maybe it would either play in her favor, or it would make her feel worse.

She hesitated as she sat there, holding her phone in her hands. She then pressed the button dialing her mother, and after hearing the ringing one a few times, she heard her mother's voice.

"There you are. So, how did it go? Should I be making arrangements for you to get a job here at the family business?" she asked.

Shelby tensed the moment she heard her mom. She didn't want her mother to think she was that weak, but she also knew that this would probably be awkward for them.

"Well hello to you too mom. And I'm doing all right. I actually wanted to let you know that I got a job as a paid intern," Shelby said.

After a brief moment, her mother finally spoke.

"You're lying," she said.

"Why do you think I'm lying Mom? You obviously don't realize just how much work I've put into this," she snapped.

"I know you're lying Shelby because I can tell. You're just saying this to help offset the fact that you're not capable of doing anything. I bet you got a pity internship," she stated.

Shelby grasped the phone in her hands. She hated when her mom was like this. It was kind of a normal thing for her to deal with, but it still didn't mean that it didn't upset her every time her mom was like that.

"Mom, would it kill you to be a tiny bit nicer to me?"

"I'm just saying Shelby, you're better off getting a better job. I highly doubt that this line of work is for you. You're probably just going to get fired the first day anyway. It's a hobby, not a lifestyle. And you should know by now that keeping it as a hobby is the best thing you can do for yourself," she said.

Shelby hated this. Her mother was always like that, and it made her feel so damn inadequate. She realized over time that her mother was definitely trying to get a rise out of her, and nothing more.

"Fine, whatever Mom. If you're not going to be supportive, I don't know what to tell you. But I've finally made an impact somewhere in my life. I know it's hard for you to understand, but if you're going to continue to be like that, I'm not going to talk to you. Hope things are good for you in the future," Shelby said.

She turned the phone off and sighed. Why did her mother always do this? But she realized that her feelings for Tasha were growing as well. She wondered if Tasha hired her out of pity, or if there was something bigger there. Regardless, she was simply happy she could finally get a job doing what she loved, which was being a fashion designer.

It certainly wouldn't be easy. Shelby knew that her mother would probably continue to berate her for the time being, but she also felt it was just the beginning, that her own mother didn't understand the turmoil she went through, and that this was just her way of branching out and moving forward.

She was just elated she could work with someone. Though, the admonishing that she heard from Danica did worry her.

"Was Tasha really that cold?" she asked herself.

She really didn't know, but she had a feeling that, whatever happened next would change her life, and she would have to wait until Monday to figure out what to do, and what she would need to do next.

Chapter Four

Tasha prepared for her first internship candidate ever. She never believed she would get to the point where she would accept people like that, but here she was.

Maybe it was her own personal desire for something more, but while she was ready for this, she also feared what might happen now that she took someone on board. She never worked well with others and was nicknamed "Frigid Tasha" because she didn't really connect with anyone.

Tasha struggled to come to terms with everything that happened during that interview. On the one hand, she was happy to finally have someone else on the team, but then, on the other hand, she feared what this might become.

That Monday, she made her way over to the fashion design school. All eyes were on her, but she simply frowned, ignoring these people as much as she could. She waited for her, and then, after a bit, Shelby finally came down.

"You're late," she snapped.

"I'm sorry! I was finishing a piece and—"

"No excuses. Let's go," Tasha said.

The last thing she wanted to hear were the excuses. When she got to her car, she then opened up the passenger door. Shelby looked at it with awe in her eyes.

"What's the matter?" Tasha asked.

"Nothing. This is really happening. I'm going to be working with you as an intern," Shelby said.

"Yes, you are," Tasha stated. She started the car and began driving.

"Well, it's strange. You never accept people as intern candidates, period. So why me?" Shelby asked.

The car stopped at a light, and Tasha looked over at Shelby. She just had to go for the deep questions at the beginning, didn't she?

"You want the truth? I honestly don't know. There was something about you which was different. You didn't pretend to be some sort of cookie-cutter like most others. You have a different air to you than what I'm used to. In a sense, it's slightly different from what I normally feel, but I also like it. I really do Shelby," she said.

Shelby blushed. Tasha then continued to drive.

"So that's it? You think I'm different? You're the first person to take a chance on me," Shelby said.

"Really now? Then why did you stay in school? If I didn't step in, you'd be struggling for a crumb of work after you graduated. So why did you stay?" Tasha asked.

Shelby pondered this, and then, after a bit, she sighed. "It's been my dream, but it's a dream that I've always had issues with achieving. Mostly because of my family," she said.

"Ahh. Horrible parents?" Tasha asked.

"My dad has a family business. A small marketing firm, and they've been pushing me for years to go with them. But they've never accepted me for the person I am. I've always felt like an outcast whenever I spent time with them. Now that I'm able to finally land a job of my own, I feel happier. I feel more in control. That's why I thank you for taking a chance with me. I always felt like I had potential, but no one seemed to understand it," Shelby said.

"I understand completely," Tasha said.

"You feel this way? But you're like super good at your job and everything," Shelby said with widened eyes.

Tasha sat back, laughing in response to her words.

"God, you really are duped, aren't you? No, I'm actually not that good at what I do Shelby. I really just got lucky. I used to be a model, you know? I actually used to model my own clothes, and I was quite good at it. But I left that world a long time ago for various reasons, reasons I'd rather not go into, and since then, I've been much happier," she admitted.

"That makes sense. I'm glad you're happy," Shelby said

"The world of fashion design is cruel and cold, but it keeps me away from my past, keeps me busy. Which is what I enjoy," Tasha admitted.

The feeling in her heart grew. Tasha didn't understand why she was just telling Shelby all of this right away. There was something about Shelby which made her feel comfortable. She didn't have the heart to fully trust Shelby yet. However, the fact that she even considered it made Tasha feel things she normally wasn't used to.

"Well, thanks for taking a chance with me too," Shelby said.

"You're welcome. I hope I can see the potential you really have sooner or later," Tasha said.

The silence filled the car once more as Tasha drove over to the office. it was only about a mile away, but the traffic on the way was heavy, and Tasha was used to it.

"For the first day, I'll drive you, but I highly recommend you find your own transportation from here on out. I can't just pick you up at any time," she said.

"Thank you, Tasha. I can do that. Do you want me to come after school, right?"

"Correct. Stay in school, finish your degree. Then after, we can discuss your hours and changing them," she said.

Shelby nodded and as they walked inside, Tasha flashed her badge. The people there simply nodded, and they let the duo in. Tasha didn't pay much attention to them, period, which aroused the curiosity of Shelby, and she could see it on her face.

"You're so cold to everyone but me. Why?" she asked.

"I don't really know. Probably because you don't piss me off," Tasha replied.

That was the truth of it, but she wondered if it was perhaps a little bit harsh. Shelby blushed, and then nodded.

"You're right. Thanks for taking a chance with me," she said.

"You're most welcome," Tasha replied.

They walked over to where the little cubicles were.

"So, this is where you'll be working. I'll give you a few pieces to draft. The first thing I want is to see what you can come up with. From there, we'll collaborate. I'm excited to be working with you Shelby," Tasha said.

"You mean that?" Shelby asked.

"But of course. You're quite interesting. Although you're nervous as hell, it's also kind of cute to see," Tasha replied.

She didn't understand why Shelby made her feel this way, but she'd be lying if she didn't like it.

"Well, the feeling is mutual Tasha. Thank you for everything you've done so far. I'll try to be the best person I can be for this job," Shelby said.

"I know you will be. I'm excited to see what you can come up with. You're quite interesting Shelby, and I really like that you're interested in this as well," Tasha said.

For a long time, she didn't move. She liked hearing Shelby's support, and was interested in what she would have to offer. But Tasha had no intention of taking this any further than she already was. This was just a business friendship, and she knew more than anything that if she took this beyond that, it would all be ruined.

But she did have a strange yearning in her body, and her heart kept gravitating toward Shelby. She didn't understand why, but at the same time, she was also quite content with the way things were, and she definitely didn't want to worry about any of this either.

Would this internship work? She didn't even know, but she was going to trust Shelby, even if in her heart and mind there was doubt, saying this could not work out.

Chapter Five

When Shelby got to the office, the first thing she expected was to be thrown into an office to do paperwork. But in this office was a dress form and supplies. The weird thing was, there was no one else around.

Guess she really was all alone here.

"What's my first project then?" Shelby asked.

"I want you to look at the magazine on the table. It's the upcoming spring collection. I would like for you to design a dress that fits into the collection. I won't assign anything else until it's done," Tasha said.

"But wait, is there anything—"

"No Shelby. I want to test our creativity. I want you to build something you can be proud of," Tasha said simply.

She walked off, leaving Shelby at the desk, still unsure of what this even meant for her.

This was the first time she ever had this much freedom regarding a job. Maybe it was because Tasha didn't fully trust her or something, but she felt both relieved, and yet, a little bit apprehensive in the process. She looked over at the desk, trying to decipher what this even meant.

The magazine had a few pictures of women on the cover, a couple of them in pretty pink dresses, but some of them in more staid colors. She flipped to Tasha's spread, and that was when she noticed it.

It was different from the rest. While in all of the other pictures, they had the same, generic "model" look to them, hers had women smiling. There were candid images of a couple sitting around talking and two women shopping. There was also a part with two women in an embrace, showing off the designs that she created.

Shelby blushed. She doubted that Tasha swung that way, but it was nice seeing that kind of representation.

"So, most of it is pretty staid, but the faces show emotion. Maybe I should follow that same pattern?" she asked.

She didn't think clothing that didn't convey emotion would sit well with Tasha. She thought about what she liked and focused on that. She liked showing love within her projects, and she always had a penchant for pinks and purples.

She decided to sketch this out, fumbling at the desk for a little while. The fact that Tasha was the only designer of the entire line was both interesting and a little bit sad. It was impressive too, but the fact that she didn't trust anyone made Shelby feel bad.

"I wonder if she will trust me after I finish this," she muttered.

Shelby highly doubted it. She already knew Tasha was judging her for all of this, but she didn't know just how heavily she was. As she finished with the initial draft, she looked at the dress form.

Shelby felt like she was overthinking all of this, like she had her mind focused on so much, when in reality it was much simpler than she was expecting it to be.

She continued to mull on this, trying to figure out where to go with it, but then, she closed her eyes. She imagined what this might be, and soon, she started to cut out the pieces, bringing them together.

Shelby had no idea what she was even planning to make. But instead she let her heart be her guide. As she continued to put this together, her mind was transfixed on this project, and this project alone. She didn't even notice anyone else, instead only focusing on the job at hand, and always making sure to leave her own touch on this item.

For Shelby, this was a big project, and it made her anxious. When she finished it at the end of the night, there was something about it that made her blush.

She paged for Tasha. After a few minutes, Tasha came down to the office. She walked toward the entrance, then stopped.

"Is this what you came up with?" she said.

"Yes. Is it bad?" Shelby asked. She looked over at the dress form, and then, back at Tasha.

Tasha's eyes were as wide as saucers, her whole body straight. Her eyes didn't leave the dress form, which had a beautiful pink and purple dress on it. The ruffle texture of it, combined with the form-fitting nature of the pink pieces, offered both an elegance and sexiness to it too.

"Did you look at anything for inspiration?" Tasha asked.

"No, I didn't," Shelby replied.

"The dress is amazing!"

Shelby's eyes immediately widened at those words. Was she serious? Shelby didn't quite comprehend that Tasha meant what she said. She wasn't lying as she uttered them.

"I followed my heart Tasha. I didn't really have much to go off of. I saw the way the people looked in those photographs, and it inspired me to show love through clothing," Shelby said.

"I don't understand. Your portfolio was complete trash, but this is a wow. I don't know how I managed to get someone so good from a school where the same person couldn't even build a decent portfolio piece," Tasha said.

Shelby blushed.

"I don't get it either. I guess it was just what my heart wanted to show. So, can you use this?" Shelby asked.

"Of course. I'm just surprised it worked out. I normally have terrible luck with people who join my team," Tasha said.

"Have you really never had an intern before?" Shelby asked.

"No. I don't work well with others. I've had people who helped me with the sales aspects of my company, but the actual work was left to me for a good reason," Tasha explained.

"Why is that?" Shelby asked.

There was a pause. Then, Tasha shook her head.

"I'd rather not discuss that right now," she muttered.

"You don't have to hide from me Tasha. I'm—"

"Shelby, if you know what's good for you, don't continue to meddle in affairs you're not supposed to meddle in. It's not good for you," Tasha snapped.

Shelby looked at her with widened eyes as Tasha left the room. Shelby didn't really understand the tension that was there, but she knew whatever Tasha was going through, she wanted to be supportive.

The cold woman had cracks in her façade. Shelby could feel it starting to crumble. She did appreciate the older woman, but she knew that Tasha had her own trauma to overcome. At that moment, perhaps it was best if she didn't pursue it any further. It could cost Shelby her job.

Shelby wanted to be there for Tasha, but at the same time, Shelby knew better than to meddle in the private affairs of another.

Chapter Six

Tasha left the room, confusion present on her face, and uncertainty in her heart and body.

"Why do I feel like this?" Tasha asked.

When she saw the dress, a strange feeling practically overtook her as she looked at the garment. It looked average compared to other dresses she saw others do, but the emotions it conveyed, the feeling of love, opened up a strange piece of Tasha that she had long since removed.

"Why did I have to think about that now?" she asked herself.

She knew that mulling on this wasn't the best answer, but Tasha would be dammed if she continued to hold back her feelings.

It reminded Tasha of her past, and not in the way that she liked being reminded.

She went to her office, grimacing as she went to her desk, trying to grapple with those feelings.

"I could just fire her right now. She'd be upset, but it might be for the best," Tasha said.

No, that would only make it messier. Shelby was already known as the person who recently got hired onto the team. If she fired her right away, it would only make things ten times worse.

Tasha couldn't do that, she just couldn't. She felt if things continued down this path, she'd be screwed.

Tasha had a lot on her mind, then her phone rang. She picked it up, holding it to her ear.

"Yes?"

"Hi Tasha, it's Pierre. Just wanted to see how your new intern was doing?" he said.

"Fine. Why do you care?"

"I was going to let you know, if you want to put something together for the fashion show next weekend, a spot has been opened. Perhaps you can work with your new creator," Pierre purred.

"I'll see. I wouldn't mind submitting something, but I don't know if I should," she admitted.

"Why? Don't you want to get your name out?"

Pierre had a point. Tasha wanted to spread the word of her fashion line, but there was also that part of her which feared what might happen.

It was mostly that fear of what would happen between Shelby and her. Shelby was a nice woman, and she was good at conveying emotion, even if her designs kind of sucked, but there was just something about everything that was going on.

"I don't know Pierre. She's very good at her job, but there's something about that which bothers me," she admitted.

"Why? You're not used to this?" he asked her.

"No, I am not used to this kind of thing. I always feel like...like I'm kind of just watching life go by, like I'm just here. But when I saw her own work, something changed within me. I don't want to put much stock in it, but I do fear this arrangement somewhat. Don't tell Angela that; she'd probably use it against me," Tasha said.

Pierre may be a rival designer, but he was also one of the few people that didn't bother her whatsoever.

"I understand the pain Tasha. I'd say the best thing for you to do, is follow your heart and make it work," he stated.

"I know. I'll try to," Tasha said.

"I believe in you Tasha. I know it's not easy, but I do believe it'll all be okay," he said.

"I just hope that things get a little bit better. When I saw her work, it reminded me of old times. And while that was nice, I didn't like it because of other reasons," Tasha said.

"Oh yes. Her," Pierre muttered.

"So, you know how I feel. I guess it's just better to keep the cold façade up. People like that side of me better," Tasha said.

"It's wrong to deny your feelings, Tasha. If there is something you must say, then say it. Plus, who knows? Love is strange. You might end up getting something more out of it than you expected," he said with a purr.

"Don't put that much stock in me please. I just want a normal life, and I want to finally acknowledge the feelings I have without it being weird for me. It's much harder than you'd think," she muttered.

"I know. I've been there before," he replied.

"Thanks Pierre. I do appreciate all that you've done for me and listening. I'll consider the spot in the show. Let me see how things go with her first and foremost," Tasha said.

"Sure, but remember, you don't have to avoid your feelings. Sometimes, it works better this way," he said.

"Right, well, I'll talk to you later," Tasha said.

Tasha hung up and put her head in her hands, sighing. She wanted to do this, but at what cost? What was the price she'd have to pay for this? She figured it would be much larger than what she was used to, and for Tasha, there was a lot of worry in her mind, and a lot of fear that enveloped her body.

She liked the idea of being able to fully understand herself, but she also knew she had a lot of trauma that came from her past; trauma she kept under wraps for a reason. She feared getting Shelby involved would open up those wounds again.

But she was a fashion designer, first and foremost. She wanted to, no matter what, make this work. She did know that, once she managed to do this, she couldn't go back to the world she always knew and loved.

Yet, in a sense she wanted to get Shelby involved. There was that part of her that craved getting Shelby to join her, to build a better fashion line.

Sure, she had people who handled all the logistical aspects of it. Up until now, she was the only designer out there, and it made her feel safe and secure. Now, she took on another, opening her up to whatever would happen next.

"I guess I should tell her," Tasha said.

She walked over to the office where Shelby was putting the final touches on the dress. Tasha waited a moment for Shelby to notice her, but then after a minute or so, she spoke.

"Hey Shelby," Tasha said.

"Hello there Tasha. What do you need?" Shelby asked.

"I came here to tell you that I...I want you to work on a fashion show piece for me. It's the theme of love, and you've done pretty amazing conveying that feeling so far. So, could you help me?" Tasha said.

The look on her face made Tasha realize that Shelby had no experience with this kind of thing either, which made her feel slightly better about herself, and then, after a brief second, Shelby spoke.

"Sure, I'd love that Tasha," Shelby said.

Tasha smiled, knowing that this was indeed the beginning of something new, something amazing, and Shelby seemed on board for whatever it was that would happen next.

Chapter Seven

Shelby couldn't believe what she just heard.

Tasha wanted her on her side, and Shelby felt pleased to be on board with all of this. Shelby wanted to be there for Tasha, no matter what, and she felt honored knowing that Tasha wanted her to do this.

"Are you sure? I'm kind of new here and—"

"Yes. You know damn well how to convey those feelings. It's almost like...you've experienced love and romance before," Tasha said.

There was tension in the air, and judging from the forlorn look on Tasha's face, she struggled with these feelings.

"I guess love has been hard for you, hasn't it?" Shelby said.

"There's a reason I'm single, right?" Tasha said with a chuckle.

"If you ever want to talk about it, just do so. Just because we're working together doesn't mean I don't care about you," Shelby said.

She could see the slight fear in Tasha's eyes, the fact that Shelby was offering this opening her up to more vulnerabilities. But Shelby understood the feeling, the fear of the moment, and the worry that overcame her.

"Listen, you don't have to worry about me. I'd be honored to work with you. I don't have a ton of experience with love. I've had a lot of experience of dealing with people who didn't love me, but the idea of love is something I've always pined for, something I've desired," Shelby said.

"You don't say," Tasha said.

Shelby blushed as Tasha sat on the chair next to her. She felt Tasha's eyes on her own, and then, Shelby sighed.

"I'm kind of a hopeless romantic. I want to find the one, the woman of my dreams, one day, but I doubt that'll happen. I don't know how to talk to women for starters, and I always feel like deep down...it's an unattainable dream, you know?" Shelby said.

She had a lot of feelings about love. It was something she wanted, mostly because she knew that some people who were close to her struggled with love.

"I understand that Shelby. I kind of...am the same way. I've closed my heart to love for a reason, but I do hope one day, I can find the one too. There's just...a lot that goes through my head when I think about love, and I always struggle with this," Tasha explained.

Shelby was surprised that Tasha felt the same way, but she nodded.

"I guess the feeling is mutual then," Shelby said with a smile on her face.

"That it is Shelby. I'm quite glad that you get that," Tasha said.

The tension filled the air. Shelby felt that strange urge to kiss her. But she stopped herself. She knew those feelings in this line of work would make it messy.

"Anyway, you want to work on this together, right? I can come in after classes each day and we can work on the pieces together," Shelby replied.

"Yes, I'd like to work on this together. If that isn't too much of an issue for you," Tasha said.

Shelby nodded.

"It shouldn't be an issue at all, I just don't want to make you uncomfortable or anything. I kind of know a little bit about what to make, but I know we both have...markedly different ideas, so it might be a little bit weird for us," Shelby said.

"I think we can come to a nice little compromise," Tasha said.

Shelby felt her eyes on her body, and Shelby couldn't help but flush. She expected Tasha to tell her she was on her own, or not even bother to work together. Yet, here she was doing this, and it made Shelby realize her own life, her own humanity, and everything that was going on.

"So, should we begin today, or wait till tomorrow so we can have fresh eyes for this?"

"Let's start tomorrow," Tasha said.

"All right. You know Tasha, you come off as very tough, but you're not that bad of a person. I can see it," Shelby said.

"Whatever. Head on out. I don't want to keep you waiting for too long," Tasha replied.

Shelby smiled, feeling a rush of excitement as it hit her body. She quickly left the office, heading to her home. Of course, as soon as she got there, she saw the missed call from her mom.

"Great, she's bothering me again," Shelby muttered, feeling her shoulders slump.

She dialed her mother, and after a few rings, her mother spoke.

"Finally, you called back," she muttered.

"Sorry Mom, I was busy with my new internship. We went over a few things today," Shelby said.

"Right. Well, your father and I would like for you to see us soon. We want to see how you've been, and if working as a fashion designer is right for you," her mother said.

"I know you're trying to get under my skin mom, but I'm not dealing with that. I'm pretty glad that I have a job working with Tasha, and we're working on a piece together," Shelby said.

"Well, I guess I'm happy for you then. You should have a backup in case everything with Tasha doesn't work out. You never know, you could get fired on the spot for just existing. You know how those types are," her mother said.

"Mom, you don't know anything," Shelby said.

"Yes, I do. I know, and I don't want you to fall into the trap of fame and fortune. Remember, I did that a long time ago," her mother replied.

Shelby knew she'd bring that up again.

"Mom just be supportive. I'm not going to meet some random man who will knock me up. Besides, you should know I'm better than that," Shelby said.

"Right, well I'm just trying to warn you. I care about you Shelby. It's why I bother you about it," her mother stated.

"Fine, whatever. I'll talk to you later," Shelby replied.

She quickly hung up the phone, feeling the cloud of doom flood over her. She was finally doing what she wanted, finally had a job that made her happy, but she was still getting crap from her mom.

It pissed her off. She knew why her mother acted this way. The pain from the past still hung over her like a dark cloud, and as much as Shelby wanted to understand, at the same time, she knew that trying to convince her mother that she was excited was something that would be much harder than she thought.

Still, for the first time in a long time, Shelby was happy when she went home that night, she felt a bit of relief. She wasn't worrying about the next school project, or what the hell she was doing after graduation.

When she was around Tasha, being in her presence made Shelby feel elated, delighted by everything, and she knew that, no matter what, everything would indeed be fine. She was happier when she was with Tasha. It was difficult at times, but she felt better than before.

The next day, she went into the classroom, feeling hyped for the next day. A couple of people looked at Shelby with surprise, and even Danica had widened eyes of curiosity.

"Is everything all right?" she asked.

"Oh yes. I feel wonderful," Shelby said.

"Really? Why?"

"I'm just doing so much better than before; nothing can bring me down. I did talk with my mom last night. She was pissed off. But I feel good. I feel confident in my life," Shelby said.

"That's good at least. Is Tasha nice?"

"Somewhat. We get along, even though she's so different. It's very weird for me, because I'm so used to dealing with people who don't really like me, who don't care, and to have someone who even shows a little bit of support is nice," Shelby said.

"That's good. I'm glad for you, Shelby. I'm glad you could secure a future for yourself. Are you doing any shows with her?"

"We're going to try to work together on a fashion show project. I don't know how this will go, but we'll see," she said.

"Good luck."

Shelby was counting down the hours till she could see Tasha again. It was strange, she didn't have any feelings for her besides that of happiness, and that made her feel confident and strong as well.

After class was over, she raced over to Tasha's office. It made her happy knowing that she had someone who took a chance on her. For being someone who had talent, she was cast to the side way too goddamn much. But she wondered if those feelings she had would ever go away.

She didn't see Tasha as anything more than a boss who she connected with. While Tasha was a gorgeous woman, Shelby knew better than to grapple with those feelings, to worry about them all that much. She could have someone who cared enough about her to want her around.

Chapter Eight

Tasha felt strangely excited for Shelby to get here. She worked on designing a few prototype projects, but for the main project, she wanted Shelby to be here. It was strange for the first time; she actually wanted the other person around.

Tasha was known for working alone. She never even had other people from the office around when she worked here, but she clamored for Shelby to show up. When she finally did, Tasha kept to herself, but then, the two of them started to work together on the projects that they had.

Shelby had some amazing ideas. Although most of the time they didn't fully match what Tasha wanted, hearing the passion in her voice made Tasha's heart melt.

"You're so passionate. Though, your designs are nothing like what the fashion world likes, you stick by them," she said.

"Well, you either stick to your buts, or continue to lie to yourself, and I am not a fan of lying," Shelby replied.

Tasha stopped, thinking about that time, back then; the reason she quit modeling. It hung over her like a knife.

"I see. Well, keep it up," Tasha said.

Shelby smiled, and Tasha felt her heart flutter as she listened to Shelby's ideas. Why did Shelby make her feel this way? Why did this make her heart thump in the way that it did? She pondered this, and after their first day working together, Shelby thanked her before leaving.

Tasha was excited, but she also felt a bit lost. After her time with Shelby, she quickly went over to the bar next to her office. She was a regular here, but she didn't like people knowing she used alcohol as a sort of crutch.

"Hey there," Nate, the bartender said.

"Hey Nate. The usual, please," Tasha said.

"Coming right up. Hey, are you okay?"

"Yes. I'm just working on trying to figure out if I made the correct decision hiring Shelby or not," Tasha muttered.

"Why? Is she horrible?" Nate asked.

"Not at all. She's perfect and I don't know how to feel about this. I've never felt this way before. This person is so different from the people I've worked with, and they're making me question myself. You know, crap like that," Tasha said.

"I say if you feel happy, don't worry so much about it, Tasha. There's probably a reason why you feel the way you do. It probably brought up some old feelings, and you're afraid of admitting that those feelings held you back for so long," Nate said.

"You may be right. I think it's best if I don't get involved with her. She doesn't need to be involved with me. I'm too cold for her, got too much baggage," Tasha explained.

"Maybe the secret is she does too, and you're made for each other. Birds of a feather, right?" he said.

"I guess," Tasha replied.

The bar was quiet, and Tasha continued to sip her drinks, getting drunker quicker. That was when the feelings came forward.

"Why do I feel this way about this damn young woman? Seriously, I hate it," Tasha said.

"Maybe those are feelings of love and affection you've long held back," Nate explained.

"I don't know if I should even act on them. You know what happened before. It's better for me to just keep everyone at a distance," Tasha replied.

"Exactly," Nate explained to her.

"Why can't I just let it go? Why do I feel the urge within me?" Tasha asked.

"Maybe those foreign feelings are something you can't escape. I say do what makes your heart skip a beat. If it means that you tell her how you feel, then do that. Otherwise, understand that you're going through a change because you've never experienced this, or maybe you've hid those feelings for a while," Nate told Tasha.

Tasha sat there, ruminating on this. She did go through this before, but the trauma was enough to make her not want to get anyone else involved.

"You're right. I guess I'll wait and see what happens," Tasha said.

"You're good. Trust me, it's hard to grapple with feelings like this. Love is strange," he said.

Tasha didn't think she was in love, not by any means, but she certainly had her own personal reasons for not totally understanding everything and working to improve on herself and make things better.

The next week felt like it went on forever. Every time she was anywhere near Shelby, Tasha felt her heart race. She didn't understand it; why did this continue to happen?

Unless, it was just the realization of those feelings she had kept at bay and kept under wraps. She felt a bit nervous about everything at hand, and she wanted nothing more than to hide those feelings forever. Shelby was a nice woman, and every single conversation with Tasha made her want to run away, because it exposed her to feelings she wasn't used to.

One night, about two weeks into the internship, Tasha got up after they finished the finishing touches.

"That looks good," she said.

"Thanks. I'm glad we could do this together, design something so amazing. I've had a wonderful time working for you Tasha," Shelby said.

"Likewise," Tasha said.

She got up and walked off, but then, Shelby spoke.

"Why do you always leave so suddenly after we've finished a part of the dress? Every time we do, you're always storming out of there. Did I do something wrong?" she asked.

Shelby looked at Tasha with that gaze, causing Tasha to bite her lip. An awakened desire roamed through her, and she wanted nothing more than to just tell Shelby the truth, but she feared what might happen if she did.

"It's nothing. Seriously," Tasha said.

"It's definitely not just *nothing*, you're worried about something. I totally did something wrong, and

I'm so sorry if I did. I guess I really am kind of a mess," Shelby said.

"No, you're fine. I'm sorry if I was a little cold toward you. I've had a lot on my mind," Tasha said.

"If you want, we can talk about this, and we can discuss this together," Shelby said.

Tasha tensed, wondering if she did just show Shelby how she felt, rather than tell her, would this work.

"There is something I've wanted to give you for a while. I know it's forbidden, but I can't stop thinking about it. It's driving me mad, and I want to tell you everything," she said, her voice quivering in response.

"You can. Nobody is stopping you, Tasha," Shelby pointed out.

Tasha felt a bit nervous because she feared the repercussions if she did take things too far; if she did decide to just say screw it and show her emotions. Would it scare Shelby? Or would she accept it because she felt the same way.

Tasha walked over, grasping Shelby's chin, and looking at her with dark eyes. She prayed this would work.

"Close your eyes. I have something to give you," she said.

Shelby looked at Tasha with wide eyes, but then, she did as she was told. Tasha felt her body move on its own, pressing her lips to Shelby's, kissing her passionately and without any faults. The two of them spent forever kissing, making Tasha happy, and embracing the feelings that Shelby gave to her.

Everything felt perfect. Tasha would be dammed if she walked away after doing this.

48

Chapter Nine

Shelby couldn't believe it.

Was Tasha really gay?

She didn't know what to do the moment she felt Tasha's lips against her own, but she quickly kissed her, and she moaned in response. She accepted the kiss, their mouths and tongues moving with a tandem that made them both groan in pleasure. Shelby couldn't believe how good this felt, and she could tell that Tasha was enjoying this too.

Tasha then pulled back, looking at Shelby with widened eyes, and with a slight look of fear on her face.

"I'm so, so damn sorry," Tasha said.

"For what Tasha? You're obviously expressing your feelings. I had a feeling you had some sort of feelings for me, but I didn't want to pressure you or anything," Shelby said.

She had been waiting for this kiss too, and she was excited to feel Tasha's lips against her own. For a long time, the two of them stayed, neither of them wanting to move, but then, Shelby pulled away.

"Sorry about that," Tasha said.

"No. It makes sense in a way," Shelby said.

"I'm sorry Shelby, I just can't stop thinking about you. It's weird for me, because I don't open my heart, but here I am, kissing you," she said.

"It's fine, Tasha. I'm a bit surprised myself at my actions, but in a way, it makes total sense," Shelby said.

"I'm glad," Tasha replied.

For a second, neither of them said anything. But then, Tasha blushed, speaking.

"You know I meant it when I kissed you," she admitted.

Shelby flushed.

"I did too. I'm really bad with this. I've liked women for a long time, but never had a girlfriend before," Shelby admitted.

"Same here. It's different, but I like it," Tasha replied.

"You've never had a girlfriend? I thought you had one a long time ago," Shelby said.

"No, she was never on my side. She wasn't really a lover. She's nothing," Tasha said.

Shelby could feel the tension from her words, making her realize that whomever it was that Tasha associated with in the past, it made her upset.

"I'm sorry if I tore open old wounds but I do like you, Tasha. A lot," Shelby admitted.

"The feeling's mutual," Tasha replied.

"May I kiss you?" Shelby asked.

Tasha looked at her for a moment, and Shelby was about ready to accept rejection, when Tasha smiled.

"You really do mean what you say, don't you," she teased.

"I do Tasha. I really do," Shelby replied.

They looked at each other, and for a long time, they just stared. But then, Shelby moved down toward Tasha, kissing her slightly. Tasha quickly responded, kissing her back, and for a long time, they both stayed like that. Tasha pushed Shelby against the wall, deepening the kiss. There wasn't anyone else around, so they could do this together, and Tasha definitely seemed to want this too. Shelby felt completely nervous and awkward, since it was her first time, but she accepted the kiss, the touches that Shelby bestowed to hers, and the pleasure that tingled within her body.

Shelby soon began to feel Tasha's lips touch the very edge of her mouth, and Tasha pushed her tongue forward, begging Shelby for entrance. Shelby quickly moaned nodding and opening her mouth a little bit to let Tasha in. Their tongues did a passionate dance. The way their muscles touched made Shelby begin to feel hot.

She was nervous, but she trusted Tasha. Even if things got awkward, or went sour, she trusted her. The coldhearted woman seemed to only show affection to Shelby, which surprised her, but at the same time, it made utter sense

For a long time, they just kissed. Then, Shelby felt her body move backwards slightly, and Tasha began to move her lisp down her neck, lightly kissing and touching there.

Shelby let out moans that she didn't even know existed within her. Tasha simply smirked at the delicious sounds she uttered.

"You sound so damn cute," Tasha said.

Shelby blushed, but not before Tasha started to lightly nibble on the neck, touching slightly. Shelby started to gasp, crying out, and gripping the edge of the wall.

She was at the mercy of Tasha's touches, and she wouldn't have this any other way.

Every time Tasha touched her body, grasping her hips and moving up to the dress shirt she wore, Shelby felt like she was in heaven. Tasha did most of the work. Even the smallest of touches was turning Shelby on, and she couldn't handle it.

Tasha started to breathe heavily too, and Shelby knew the desire within Tasha's eyes was real. Tasha then started to move her hands toward the sides of the dress shirt, pulling it off over Shelby's head and refencing her perky breasts. Shelby blushed as Tasha's hands trailed down her body, touching every little crevice. Her hands moved toward each round orb, squeezing it slightly, and smiling.

"You have wonderful breasts. I'm a little jealous," Tasha said.

"Thank you," Shelby said with a blush.

Suddenly as quick as it happened, Shelby then felt the hand move from her breasts to the back of her bra, undoing the clasp and pulling the garment off. Shelby gasped as the cold air hit her nipples, causing them to perk in response.

"Aww, so perky and cute," Tasha said with a purr.

Shelby flushed, but not before Tasha began to move her lips toward the very tip of the nipple, touching and pressing her lips to the very edge of it. She kissed the tip, making Shelby cry out in pleasure as she sucked on the bud, touching the tip of the nipple and making Shelby gasp in pleasure. Everything about this was making Shelby go crazy, and as Tasha continued to touch and tease the little bud, she couldn't help but love everything about this.

It was making Shelby go crazy, and she couldn't believe how sensitive her nipples even were. She loved every moment of this, and with each touch, Tasha made her tense up.

Tasha seemed to know what she was doing, at least more than her. She felt Tasha move her lips downwards, touching and kissing her slightly. As she continued the downward motions, Shelby groaned, feeling her body ache for more.

There wasn't anyone else around the office. Shelby was grateful for that, because the last thing she wanted was for someone to hear her. Tasha pushed her toward the desk, spreading her legs apart, and moving her skirt up.

The hungry look in Tasha's eyes made Shelby blush, the excitement only growing more so within her. She ached for more, craved the feeling of Tasha's touch, and Tasha simply smiled.

"You enjoying this, cutie?" she asked.

"Yes. Please. I want more," Shelby said, her body aching for this.

Shelby felt like Tasha seemed to understand exactly what to do to make her feel good, and she enjoyed that immensely. Tasha then moved down toward the apex between her legs, kissing up the edge of her thigh with small, succulent kisses. Every single touch, every single motion, it all made Shelby cry out and beg for more, the pleasure of the moment aching within her.

Shelby enjoyed this, and she knew that Tasha was liking everything that was happening too. Every single touch made Shelby beg for more, and when Tasha got between her legs, rubbing her there, she started to look into Shelby's' eyes. Shelby began to cry out, holding her hips up and forward, enjoying every single moment of this. She craved this feeling, craved this touch, and it was enough to make her beg for more from Tasha.

Tasha seemed to know what to do then because she rubbed faster. Shelby gripped the sides of the desk, moaning aloud, enjoying every single motion and touch from Tasha's hands. Tasha finally pulled her panties down, releasing her aching, throbbing womanhood. Tasha spread her apart, using her tongue to tease her slit with the littlest touches.

Shelby's eyes widened, feeling the shock of the moment, enjoying everything that came from this. She knew that Tasha was good, but not...this good. Tasha had the skills and the desire to make her feel amazing, and it was all Shelby could do not to lose her mind right then and there. Shelby started to cry out, aching for the feelings that came from this, and she wanted nothing more than to just feel this entire moment.

After a bit, Tasha touched that spot, that one location which made Shelby scream out, suddenly tensing up, and then, she relaxed, feeling the thrill of the orgasm.

Shelby looked over at Tasha, who smiled at her, giving her a kiss. Shelby could taste herself on there, and while it was a different taste, she didn't mind it.

"You good?" Tasha asked.

"Amazing," Shelby said.

"Great, I wanted to make you feel good. I've wanted to do that for a while. I don't really know why," Tasha said.

Shelby flushed, realizing that Tasha had similar feelings that she did.

"You want me to…return the favor?" she inquired with a blush.

"You don't have to if you don't want to Shelby," Tasha insisted.

"No, I want to," Shelby stated, moving toward Tasha and pulling her skirt up.

The older woman gasped, surprised at the techniques that Shelby knew. Shelby just copied what she saw in porn and romance movies, using her fingers to press inside, tease her, and using her tongue to dance around the edge of Tasha's clit. Tasha started to let out a series of husky sounds from her lips, enjoying every moment of this. Shelby watched as Tasha grasped the edge of the desk, crying out as Shelby started to push her fingers in deeper, exploring Tasha without any stops. This was all new to Shelby, but she seemed to be doing the right thing; at least she gathered as much from the sounds she heard Tasha moaning.

She spread her apart, using her tongue against that one spot again, her fingers continuing in their own skillful way. She watched as Tasha cried out, her whole body moving forward for just a moment, and then, relaxing back.

"Wow," Tasha said.

"Are you good?" Shelby inquired.

"Better than good. I'm content," Tasha said.

"I am too," Shelby replied.

For a moment, neither of them said much. Shelby wondered if this meant something. But then, as quickly as it happened, Tasha turned away.

"This doesn't have to mean anything more than it does Shelby. We can continue to have our professional relationship. I just couldn't stop thinking about you," she said.

"I mean, if you want to keep seeing each other, that's fine too. I'm glad that we can have this moment together," Shelby said.

She could tell that Tasha wasn't going to just let this go. While she normally did notice that Tasha was a bit hesitant on this, she definitely was shocked that Tasha seemed so adamant about just kind of keeping their life to what this was right now.

"I'm sorry Shelby, I'm a little hesitant about taking this further. Don't take it personally," Tasha said.

Shelby felt a bit upset. She thought that this might be something real for them, but maybe it was Tasha's own personal worries about her job or something. Either way, Shelby was just excited to experience that with her, but at the same time, she also feared whether this would turn into anything more.

As they parted ways, Shelby could tell Tasha had some thinking to do. She went back to the dress form, looking at their work.

They built this together. It was literal labor of love, and Shelby hoped that their potential and future wouldn't completely jeopardize it.

Chapter Ten

Tasha was pensive. It wasn't like she disliked Shelby. She feared the future, especially with everything that happened before.

Tasha raced to her office, slamming the door and shaking her head. She was fearful of what might come from it, from the new feelings that came from Shelby.

It reminded her of back then.

The person who she thought she loved but ended up getting assaulted by.

Tasha didn't want to bring Shelby into it. She just wanted to continue on with her life and to have closure. She wanted nothing more than to experience that, and not worry so much about the tensions of the past.

The next day, Shelby came in, and Tasha greeted her simply.

"Are you all right, Tasha?" Shelby asked.

If only she knew the truth. Shelby was so dense when it came to this, that Tasha didn't want to get too involved with her.

"I'm fine. Don't worry about me," she said.

"You know, the more you say that, the more I'll worry," Shelby pointed out.

"Don't. I'm serious I'm—"

Shelby looked over at her desk, seeing the names for the fashion show on there. There was one name that was crossed out, and it was crossed out heavily. Tasha quickly grabbed it, holding it there.

"What's the matter? What are you hiding Tasha? You can tell me," she said.

"Don't worry about it, seriously," she muttered.

"Come on Tasha, I thought maybe after we hooked up like that, you'd be more open. I guess I was wrong," Shelby said.

Tasha tensed, looking at Shelby with a look of worry on her face.

"You don't have to worry about me," she said.

"You're lying Tasha. You've got a lot of baggage, and you worry about telling others, and you'll continue to act like that until you do," Shelby said.

"Like you'd know," Tasha scoffed.

Shelby looked at her, and then, she laughed.

"What if I told you that I do, because I'm the same way whenever my family is mentioned," she said.

"No way," Tasha replied.

"Way. My family is something. My dad is a mess, my mom is a homophobe, and the two of them only care about me because they brought me into this world on accident. I was an 'oops' baby, and I have a lot of feelings about that. They're quite annoying even though I did get a better job recently," Shelby explained.

There was no way that she would understand so easily. It bothered Tasha, and it made her realize that she was definitely not alone.

"I understand. However, I don't want you to feel like you have to worry about me," she said.

"Come on Tasha. I'm not going to hate you or anything for what it is that you tell me, I'd much rather you just told me the truth," Shelby said.

Tasha paused, thinking about that. she could just be honest and tell her everything, but that may complicate her feelings.

"I'd rather not talk about it right now," Tasha said.

"But—"

"Shelby, please. If you love me, you'll not ask about this. Please," Tasha implored.

She didn't want to tell anyone else about this right now.

"Fine. I'm sorry if I bothered you too much about it. I'll be in my office," Shelby said.

"Good. We need that dress done for the fashion show, and I'm trying to set everything up for that," Tasha said.

"Fine."

Shelby walked away, leaving Tasha to sigh in frustration. She hated that Shelby left in the manner she did. Tasha hated telling the truth about her feelings. Mostly since she didn't know how to feel about any of it. She looked at the sheet, seeing the crossed-out name like it was everything.

Meryl Kline.

Meryl. It was her ex-girlfriend. She used and abused Tasha as a model. She feared telling anyone the truth because Tasha didn't know if anyone would actually believe her. She also knew holding onto her feelings wasn't healthy for her either.

"I don't know what the hell I'm going to do," Tasha said.

She called Pierre. After a few rings, he spoke.

"Hey there, Tasha. Is everything all right?"

"Could be better. Who put Meryl in the lineup for the show? You know I don't like her," Tasha said.

"That wasn't me. I respect your wishes. We may be competitors, but I know what she did to you. It has to be Angela," he said.

Angela. She was always doing something to get the one-upmanship over others.

"Well this isn't. Can you try talking to her? I know if I say anything, I'll probably get some crap from her," Tasha said.

"True. I don't know why. Maybe she's working with Angela," Pierre said.

"But Angela should know better than to agree to having her. This is annoying," Tasha said.

"I'll see if I can talk to her. Meanwhile, don't get too worked up about it. It happens, and I'm sure that once you work this out, everything will be fine," Pierre said.

"It's much easier said than done Pierre, but thanks," Tasha said.

She hung up the phone, sighing in annoyance. This was the last thing she wanted. She was finally trying to move on, and that was there. She wanted to just get the answers there, but she didn't know how. For now, she'd wait and see, and hopefully, she didn't need to worry about Meryl being there.

At least, that was what she wished for.

Chapter Eleven

Shelby walked off, feeling frustrated by the way Tasha was acting toward her. She didn't understand, why was Tasha acting so off all of a sudden?

Shelby wanted to ask why, to find out why Tasha acted the way that she did, but each time she thought about asking, she felt a little guilty about it. She didn't want to make her uncomfortable, she just…hated that she didn't have any answers to anything that was happening. It made her wonder if she could even help her, or if it was better if she just stayed in her own place.

The next day, Shelby went to school, and Danica was nearby.

"Hi, Shelby. How is everything with Tasha?"

"All right. She's been acting strange," Shelby said.

"Uh oh. Did something happen between you two?'

"No. Not bad or anything. She's just been distant. Something happened, and since she mentioned that, she's been off. I don't really know what to say, other than to be supportive when I can," Shelby admitted.

Shelby hated that Tasha acted this way toward her, but it wasn't like she could just beg for her to tell her what's wrong.

"I can tell you're upset. I mean, if you need to talk about it with anyone, I'll listen. I know how it can be, stressing over internships. I got accepted to one, but the person is a total asshole," Danica admitted.

"I just don't know. I think she's hiding her emotions, and I want to help, but I don't want to trouble her," Shelby said.

"I can tell Tasha doesn't like speaking about how she feels. The best thing for you to do there Shelby, is be honest. Tell her what you're feeling and see for yourself what happens next. She may tell you. But I don't think ignoring the situation will help, whatever it might be," Danica pointed out.

"She won't even tell me or anything," Shelby admitted.

"Maybe you should confront her. I wouldn't suggest trying to go through her office and finding out the truth. It seems she's guarded and won't let anyone know," Danica said.

"It's the last thing I want to do. I'm stressed about this big design we have for the Spring Fashion Show coming up next week. I want to do something my parents will be proud of," Shelby admitted.

After she spoke with Danica, she went to class. It all felt so boring when she wasn't around Tasha. When she finally got to Tasha's place, Tasha was there, but she was quiet.

"Hey there," Shelby said.

"Hey. I don't think I'll be needing you today," Tasha said.

"Why is that? I know we finished the dress but are there any other pieces we have to work on? We have a whole line. I thought I was part of the team," Shelby said.

"Well, I'd prefer to work alone right now, Shelby," Tasha said.

Shelby looked at Tasha, holding her hands to her hips and glaring at the woman.

"Why do you insist upon acting like that?" Shelby inquired.

"Like what?"

"Like whatever this is. This strange sort of behavior is so unbecoming of you, and I hate it," Shelby said.

"You're talking about why I don't want to get into all the details of the whole mess with the fashion show, right? Well, there's a problem on my end I must handle, but I don't want you to get involved," Tasha said.

"You're always acting like that these days. Ever since I came in after we did what we did that night, you've been distant. You don't regret it do you?" Shelby asked.

Tasha paused. Shelby immediately felt her heart sink. She didn't know what to say but realizing that Tasha did regret what she did made her realize her place.

"I don't want to get into it, Shelby. I'm serious," Tasha said.

"You're lying. Why don't you just tell me? I know it's bothering you, but I'm not going to just sit there and expect that you'll just let me know everything. I want you to be open with me. Or was I just another person to fuck, another sorry sucker who got conned into your life?" Shelby asked.

"No, that's not it Shelby! It's a lot more than that. I just have a lot going on," Tasha said.

"Why can't you tell me then?"

Tasha then hesitated, and Shelby scoffed.

"I knew it. You didn't see me as anything more than a fuck buddy that night. I guess that's it. I'm just a fuck buddy and someone who helps you with your designs. You know, I think I need a little bit of time away from here myself. I'm going to take a break for a bit," Shelby said.

"But Shelby you're—"

"If you're just going to toss me to the side the moment I show any compassion for you, I think it's better if I do stay away," Shelby replied.

Her eyes were filled with tears as she uttered those words.

She knew that this wasn't what Tasha wanted. For now, it was better this way. If Tasha were to keep hiding these secrets, Shelby would live her own life, and not get involved.

When Shelby got out of there, her phone rang, and as she picked it up, she heard the sounds of labored breathing.

"Mom? Is everything all right?"

"Your father. He's in the hospital right now."

Chapter Twelve

Tasha thought about what she did. Was it the right thing?

It's not like she could go back and take back what she said to Shelby. She knew she screwed up, and that not telling her everything made it worse. It made her wonder if she even did the right thing with Shelby.

Keeping her in the dark was only making things worse. She feared if she did let her in, and they grew closer, it could affect their relationship.

After a little bit, Tasha went back to work. She was putting some trimmings on a cute skirt and sweater combo, but as she did it, she realized...it felt empty, hollow and boring.

She didn't really know what else to do, other than to just work on this. But, as she did it, she realized it didn't feel the same as it did when she had Shelby helping her.

When they did this, they would make small talk, little jokes, or comment on the piece. But everything felt hollow. For the first time, Tasha regretted she was designing everything alone.

Everything felt so hollow and boring, that by the time she finished it, she looked at it and scoffed.

"This looks like crap. I'm going to have to redo it," Tasha said.

She looked at the other pieces she made with Shelby, and they all felt different. Did it really matter all that much that two people were working on this together? Apparently so, because there was a stark difference in this too.

Tasha wished she could just tell Shelby the truth, but maybe it was the right thing to do to keep her in the dark. That was best because she wouldn't have to get hurt, and she didn't need to worry about protecting another. But, in her mind, she wondered if she did the right thing.

"I need a fucking drink," Tasha said.

When she went over to the bar, she stepped inside, seeing Nate there. When she sat down, he poured her a scotch, and she drank it.

"You knew what I wanted from the moment I walked in," Tasha teased.

"I could see it on your face. You're stressed about whatever is going on in your life. You're concerned about her," he said.

"You mean the woman? I was a bitch to her. I needed space. But, right now, I'm just worried. I don't really know what else to do at this point besides just accept everything. All of my designs feel bland and boring, and I feel like I'm missing something," Tasha said.

"Maybe you should tell her. Maybe this is a sign that you like her," he said.

"I doubt it. I don't know if I should or not. I don't want to mess this up. I did in the past. I opened my heart, and I got hurt," Tasha admitted.

"You do realize that the past is the past. You don't need to always worry about that," he said.

"Maybe you're right. I always feel a little bit guilty," Tasha admitted.

"I know, but I think she will understand," Nate said.

"True. I don't want to lose her. It's the first time in a long time I've felt this way, and I don't want to lose this feeling," Tasha admitted.

"Do you love her?"

Love her? Tasha didn't think that, but the feelings were strong.

"Love is a strong word. I'm not really the romantic type, but I would have to say the feelings I experience for her are something extraordinary," Tasha said.

"Then maybe you should tell her. Explain it, and I mean, if she needs to work with this person too, it's only right if you're able to tell her the honest truth," he replied.

"Thank you, Nate. Hopefully, I can tell her how I really feel. She hasn't spoken to me at all. Maybe I should give her a few more days," she said.

"That might be best," he replied.

After she finished up, she headed back to her place, trying to be creative again, but failing miserably.

She needed Shelby, whether she liked it or not. After she finished up with the current projects she had, she tried to call again, but no dice.

"Where the hell is she? We've got a show coming up very soon, and I'd love it if she didn't do this right now," she said.

She tried again and again to contact her, but there was nothing. After three days, she decided to go to the school.

When she got there, she marched right into the office where the dean was.

"Hello, do you know where Shelby Morgan is? I'm Tasha Gambino, who she interns for, and I haven't seen her in a few days. We had a falling out and—"

"Oh, Shelby's isn't currently in school. She had to go see her dad," he said.

"What do you mean?" she asked.

"Shelby's dad had a bad fall. He's been doing awful. I can give you the address as well," he offered.

She immediately regretted all of the anger she felt. She didn't know Shelby's family was struggling.

"Thank you. I'd love that," she said.

"Here, I hope this helps."

She pocketed the address and made her way over. When she got there, she saw the big, sprawling entrance.

"Well, here we go. He gave me the names of her parents too. Hopefully, it'll be enough to find her," Tasha said to bolster her confidence.

She wished Shelby were more open. When Tasha got to the reception desk, she asked about Shelby's father. Tasha turned, and right in front of her was Shelby, along with a begrudging woman.

Chapter Thirteen

Shelby looked at her mom, and then at Tasha.

"Oh my God!" she said.

"Shelby, who is this?" she said.

"Shelby, are you okay? I tried to call you but—"

"Sorry Tasha. A lot happened. I've been here with my dad for a few days. He had a bad fall. It turns out he may not live long," Shelby said.

Shelby turned away, and Tasha's eyes widened.

"I'm so sorry Shelby.

"After all that happened, I thought you'd never want to see me again," she said.

"Shelby, who is this woman?" her mother asked.

Shelby blushed, turning from her mom to Tasha, and then to her mom again.

"Mom, this is Tasha. The woman who hired me for the internship."

Her mother looked at her with a judgmental look, and then back at Tasha.

"I see. So, what does she do?"

"She's a fashion designer, Mom. Can't you see?" Shelby said.

"Well, I thought you were lying, and she was a sugar mommy or something," her mother said.

Tasha's eyes widened and Shelby blushed.

"No, Mom. I really do work for her," she said.

"I see. Well, I'm glad you figured that out. We should go see your dad. So why is she here?" her mother asked.

"I came because Shelby and I had an argument before everything happened and I came over to apologize," Tasha said.

"I see. Well, I don't know how to feel about you actually being a designer there Shelby, but if she makes you happy, then continue on I guess," her mother said.

Shelby looked at her mom, who continued to glare at Tasha. "Mom, you do realize that acting won't make things better, right? It won't bring you and dad closer," she replied.

"That isn't the point," her mother snapped.

Tasha looked at Shelby, and Shelby simply nodded. She wasn't going to sit here and take all of verbal abuse from her own parent.

"No, Mom. You listen to me. I'm tired of you always acting like I'm a burden or something. I'm tired of you acting like I don't matter otherwise," Shelby said.

"But Shelby—"

"Mom, you can continue to treat me like that, but it won't make your relationship with Dad better," Shelby replied.

Tasha's eyes were wide in shock, and her mom's eyes as well.

"But Shelby, you're not making sense. We just want what's best for you," her mother said.

"No, Mom. You want what's best for yourself. You can't live with a daughter who doesn't join your family business, and who doesn't pursue a business degree. You've made me feel like crap just for being happy," Shelby replied.

Her mother looked at her. Then she looked at Tasha.

"So, Tasha's the one then? The one who's been helping you? You've been happier, and I'm glad about that, but a little jealous. With the way your father is, I'm trying my best," her mother explained.

Shelby knew this was coming, and some of the people that were around were definitely wondering what was going on.

"Listen, Mom. I'm not really mad or anything. I'm just tired of you always putting me down. I know that I'm not the best at what I do, but Tasha took a chance. So, the least you should do is listen to me," Shelby said.

Her mother looked at her, then at Tasha.

"Let's go over there and talk about this. I'm going to need some space and I don't want to talk about this in front of the doctors," her mother said.

Shelby and Tasha followed her, with Shelby looking over at Tasha, and then at her mother. When they got to the side room, she closed the door, sitting down. She threw her head in her hands.

"I'm sorry, Shelby. I really, really am," her mother said.

"What do you mean?" Shelby asked.

"I'm sorry for being such an obstacle for you. I didn't want you to go through the same thing I did all those years ago. In the past, I tried to follow my own dream of being a musician, which was how I met your father, and well, you happened. I was following a pipedream, and I didn't really sit back and look at the way everything would pan out. I felt better once I realized with the way things were, it was better for me to be realistic. I just don't want you getting hurt at all Shelby. I'm serious," her mother said.

"I know, Mom. But Tasha is definitely not just another person. She's someone special to me, and we've really connected," Shelby explained.

"I can tell."

Shelby blushed, then Tasha spoke.

"I know, as a mother, you're guarded. But, there's no need to be concerned. I have it covered," Tasha said.

"I know you do. I'm Katherine by the way. I'm her mother, and someone I wish didn't actually mess up all those years ago. I really do care about you Shelby, but I don't know if your father and I will last. I stuck around because of you, and I always wanted to show you that I meant well. I always wanted to do what's best for you, but I'm definitively not all that happy with my choices," Katherine admitted.

"So, you want to divorce him?" Shelby asked.

In a way, she knew that this was coming. It was only a matter of time, but she had a feeling that it would be like that.

"Yes Shelby, I'm going to divorce him if we can't actually make this work. If we can't, then I'm going to have to do it. For my own sanity. But I won't leave him behind in the hospital," Katherine explained.

"Because you love him," Shelby said.

"I do, I just sometimes feel like our relationship isn't the best. We could do so much more, be so much better. I think we'll need a counselor or something," Katherine explained.

"You should consider that, Mom. I'm serious," Shelby admonished.

"You do care about him. You just need a little push you know," Tasha said.

"Thank you, both of you for listening. I'm really happy about that," Katherine said.

"It's all good. I mean, you do care about Shelby. You just have a horrible way of explaining it," Tasha sad.

"I guess that's it," Katherine replied with a laugh.

There was a pause, and Katherine looked over at Shelby.

"So, Shelby, there is one thing that I'd like to ask. Something I feel is important to us," Katherine stated.

Shelby and Tasha looked at each other, and then at her mom.

"What is it, Mom?"

"Is Tasha your girlfriend? I don't want to jump to conclusions but the way you two actually spend time together, I wouldn't be surprised," she said.

Shelby and Tasha both blushed. They looked at each. Then, Shelby spoke.

"Not technically, but we're close. I don't want to jump to conclusions on that yet," Shelby said.

"I see. Well, I just wanted an answer. But, I'm glad that you're happy Shelby. I really am," she said.

Shelby blushed, and Tasha looked over at her. She immediately tensed, seeing that look on her face.

"With regards to the whole mess with my dad, you don't have to stay with him, Mom. You don't have to continue down this path. If you do end up getting a divorce, please let me see both of you at least once together before you do," Shelby said.

"Of course. I'm sorry it has to be this way Shelby, but I don't really know what to do. I have a lot on my mind, and a lot that even I don't know what to do with, and I'm glad that you're understanding," Katherine said.

Shelby and Tasha both stayed quiet, and the tension in the air was so thick, one could cut it with a knife.

"Thanks, Mom. I don't hate you. I just wish things were easier."

"I know. But, I'm here for you. I'm sorry if sometimes I come off as not being supportive," she said.

"It's fine, Mom. I don't hate you," Shelby said.

They hugged, and then after a bit, Shelby looked over at Tasha.

"Why are you here anyway? I mean, I've been here because of my dad and helping my mom. It turns out he has a brain hemorrhage, so who knows what'll happen," Shelby said.

"Oh! I wanted to talk to you about something," Tasha said.

"Sure. Is it about what happened the other night?" Shelby asked.

"Yes, about what we discussed the other night. You won't be mad if we talked about it outside of this stuffy hospital, right? I just don't want you to feel like I'm trying to hide anything from you," Tasha said.

"You can go Shelby. I'll be with your father. I'll keep you updated on everything. But Tasha seems like a good person, and someone who will take care of you. Perhaps better than I could," her mother replied.

"Thanks, Mom. I'll visit of course, but I'm glad that you…you're letting me finally make decisions on my own," she said.

"I'm trying Shelby. I really am. I just get a little paranoid because I know it's definitely not easy out there and with the way people are, I worry sometimes. But you seem happier, seem better, and I'm definitely happy to see you doing well," she said.

"Thanks Mom," Shelby replied.

They hugged, and after they finished, they all walked away. Shelby walked with Tasha, who was quiet, and when they got outside, Shelby flushed.

"I'm really sorry I didn't tell you what was going on. I was troubled," she said.

"I know," Tasha said.

"I feel horrible for not telling you the truth. What was it that you needed?" Shelby said.

Tasha pointed to the little café over in the distance. "Can we talk there? I want to do it in a more private setting, but also a place where we can discuss it like adults. It's a bit of a personal issue, something that has recently come up and has been bothering me. I don't really know what to do about it right now," she said.

"Sure, that's fine," Shelby said.

When they went inside, they sat at the booth, with Shelby looking at Tasha with a glance that screamed she wanted to know the truth about what was going on. What was biting at Tasha's behind to the point she didn't want to say it anywhere else.

"Now that we're sitting down, we can talk. There's something I've wanted to discuss with you for a while Shelby. I didn't know how to approach this without it being weird."

Chapter Fourteen

Tasha sat there trying to figure out where to take this. On the one hand, she was happy to have finally gotten the courage to say what she wanted to say, but she also feared what might happen next.

"Shelby, Meryl is a model that I knew a long time ago. Someone who I wished I didn't have to ever see again," Tasha said.

Tasha remembered that day like it was yesterday, even though it was nearly five years back. Tasha was pushing forty. She modeled until she was in her thirties. Until, the whole mess with Meryl happened.

"So, she's an old friend, I'm guessing," Shelby said.

"Friend is far from it. More like the reason why I haven't worked with anyone until you came along," Tasha admitted, sighing in annoyance.

"What happened with her? I didn't know you modeled?" Shelby pointed out.

"I did. Before I got into designing clothes, I was the one behind the magic, doing the modeling along with the designing. It's the reason I'm known as the 'woman who can do anything' according to many in the fashion world. It's because, from about age twenty-two until around my mid-thirties, I was doing everything. I've always had a knack for designing. Of course, being the tall and skinny woman that I was, it gave me the leverage to model my own clothing. I definitely was happy with that, and I was super successful. That is, until I met Meryl all those years ago," Tasha said.

"Whose Meryl? I mean, was she a friend, a rival or what?"

"At first, she was a friend. She was like you and me. We were close. I had strong feelings for Meryl. I thought she felt the same way. At first, things were great. Everything seemed perfect, like I was on cloud nine when it came to working with her. I never wanted to leave," Tasha explained.

"I can tell she meant a whole lot to you," Shelby said.

"I thought she felt the same way. She was always flirting with me and making little comments here and there. I felt it was something that would only get better with time. Then, things changed. She started to accept my advancements. Being the idiot that I was, I agreed to it. The biggest mistake of my life happened when I was about thirty. And, I still had to live with it. It was the day I told Meryl how I felt about her," she said.

"Didn't she feel that same way?" Shelby asked.

"No. Much worse. She played with my heart and made me think she cared," Tasha explained.

Tasha tensed as she thought about that day. The day she realized she was used by the person she'd fallen for.

"Did she ever care about you?" Shelby asked.

"No, I harbored a schoolgirl crush on her. I thought Meryl really cared. I talked with her from time to time. While I was pretty happy with some of the interactions, she didn't give me the time of day. Or at least, not in the way I expected it," Tasha said.

"So, what happened then?" Shelby asked.

It was the moment, the point in which the trauma would be revealed. Tasha knew for a fact that coming out with the truth would help with healing, especially with the way things were.

"Meryl immediately came onto me. She told me she wanted to see me one night, and then forced herself on me," Tasha explained.

Shelby's' eyes opened, but before Tasha said anything more, the server came over. She gave him their order, and after he quickly ran off, Tasha finally spoke.

"I told her that I liked her. But she immediately took that as I wanted to fuck her. I didn't. She manipulated me, saying this was the only way, and that I shouldn't be a baby. So, I caved. I finally agreed. She took my virginity. I was so young and vulnerable. I was confused about love and sex," Tasha explained.

She felt her body shudder in response to these words. When Shelby looked at her, she felt the feelings of regret, and the feelings from back then overtake her.

"I'm sorry if I'm being a bit much. I've never talked with anyone about this. I've considered therapists, but most of the time they give some half-hearted advice rather than actual help. Plus, I felt it was better to come clean to you now, than to let it hang over my head for a long time. I have a lot of feelings for you, and I want to be something serious. But, a part of that requires me to be honest about my past, about everything that has happened," Tasha said.

"I understand. Did it occur a lot?" Shelby asked.

"She would do it every time we were on the catwalk together. She wouldn't ever seek me out outside of that. She would play with my feelings, pretending to love me and all. She would tell me how much I meant to her, and how important I was, but then ignore me. She would lie, just to have sex with me. She would manipulate me. I still remember one time when she threatened to tell everyone about what we were doing if I didn't have sex with her. It was hard," Tasha said.

"I'm so sorry, Tasha. How come she hasn't been outed yet?" Shelby asked.

"I'm afraid to come forward. I know that I if did that, things would get worse. I knew, with the way everything was, it would only come back to bite me. I don't want to continue to hide, Shelby. I want to finally put the pain behind me," Tasha explained.

"You have to face her, Tasha. You were manipulated, hurt and you need some solace. I, for one, understand that completely," Shelby said.

"Thanks Shelby, it's really nice to have that. I want to go on the runway again. Since she threatened me, I've been scared to actually go forward on the catwalk, to actually model my own outfits. After that, I fell and just work in designing. I don't want to do that anymore. I want to be myself and do what makes me happy. The way for me to be happy would be to model my own clothing, to show off that I'm a woman of many talents, and I'm not giving up just because of some bullies in the industry," Tasha explained.

Shelby nodded, and when Tasha said those words, it felt like a weight was lifted off her body. She didn't feel bad telling Shelby everything, since Shelby seemed to get it, in her own unique way.

"You know, if you really want to, I can help fit the dress to your body, and we can practice. I mean, I don't really model myself. I'm just a designer. If it will make you happy Tasha, I'd love that," she said.

Tasha's eyes widened, her heart racing in response to the words there. "You're amazing Shelby," she said.

"Thank you dear," Shelby replied.

For a second, Tasha felt her heart melt. This was the first time she felt like she could open her heart to someone, and actually tell them the truth.

"People may question us. I'm going to be honest with you, Shelby. I don't care what people say or do; I just really want to be with you. I feel like we have something stronger," Tasha said.

Shelby blushed and Tasha felt her heart and body melt. Shelby extended her hand, and Tasha grasped it, holding it there. Tasha wasn't afraid of Meryl or her games, but rather, she felt excited for the future.

Romance was something Tasha was never all that good at, and it was something she utterly struggled with, but when she spoke with Shelby, telling her everything in life, and all of her own personal problems and worries, she felt happy and secure. She didn't feel like she had to pretend anymore, and when she was honest with Shelby, it just felt right.

"So, I think once we're done here, we should meet up tomorrow and work on this together. We have to be pretty quick. We don't have much time," Tasha said.

"That is fine with me. Did you manage to get anything done while I was gone?" Shelby asked.

Tasha laughed. "I did, but it's honestly not the same without your touch. You've got that magic tough there Shelby, and I'm glad that I have you on my team," Tasha said.

In her heart, she felt a wave of happiness, something that she normally didn't feel when she thought about work, or about life. The trauma of the past still clung to her like a burden, and Tasha knew that the only way to overcome everything would be to face her fears, to finally come forward with the truth of her abuse, and to quit holding back.

But, would it be possible? Or would she get encumbered by the feelings of the past, and unable to work on the future anymore? She didn't even know anymore, but she was just ready to see this through the end, no matter what, and she had a feeling that Shelby was the same way.

Chapter Fifteen

The next day, Shelby went over to Tasha's office once again. She felt happy once more, and while Shelby didn't really hear much from her family, she knew that her mom was definitely doing better. She did worry about her future with her dad, but Shelby knew that was their problem, not her own.

Her big problem was how madly she was falling for Tasha.

When she got into the office, she saw Tasha working on a couple of dresses. They looked decent, but she was right—they were missing her touch.

"Wow, you really did need me for this," she teased.

"I couldn't figure out what to do or anything," Tasha replied.

Shelby raced over, grasping the dress and looking it over. It needed a lot of work, and while she was willing to put the effort in, she wanted to do this with Tasha.

This was their project, and she'd be dammed if she did this all on her own.

"You definitely need a little bit of support then," Shelby teased.

"You know, that could help. Call me crazy, but it probably would do me a little bit of good," Tasha teased.

Shelby grinned, but not before she grasped the dress, holding it there, and looking it over. It definitely needed some trim updates, but she wanted to make sure this was in line with what Tasha wanted.

"Is it all right if I do a few things and then run them off you so that I'm not messing it up?" Shelby asked.

"Of course. This is our creation, something we have to do together," Tasha replied with a grin.

Shelby nodded, feeling happy with the way things were. She didn't feel like she was bothered or pressured anymore, and she definitely was quite happy with the results of it all. She definitely was much better off now than she was in the past, and it made her happy as well. Shelby began to look over some of the different parts, adding a couple of different colors. She seam-ripped a few of the troublesome areas that she didn't like as much, installing some different aspects, changing the different panels to make this work.

It was a project, and it certainly would take some time, but Shelby felt happy to help Tasha out. They continued to work on this over the next couple of weeks, until finally, the dress was finished.

Tasha put it on, grimacing slightly at the size.

"Do I need to take it out a bit?" Shelby asked.

"I'm not the same size as I used to be. But I'm used to that," Tasha said.

Shelby nodded. "I'm sure we can make this work," she said.

Shelby was quite happy with the way it was going. She saw that Tasha was happy too, something she normally wasn't used to, but something which made her feel all warm and fuzzy inside.

They worked through the night, over the next few days, to make things perfect, until finally, the entire dress line was completed. Once Shelby added the final touches, she helped Tasha put one on. The dress was a process, but when they finished, Shelby looked at it with complete awe.

"You look amazing, Tasha," she said.

Tasha looked like a goddess, in a lush array of pinks, purples, and reds. The dress looked like something out of a fairy tale, and when Tasha turned around in it, the dress billowed like an ethereal glow.

"This is just...wow," she said.

"Does it fit well?" Shelby asked.

This was her first real dress she made for someone, that she tailored to fit them, and Tasha nodded.

"I love it," she replied.

"I'm glad Tasha. I'm really glad that you can enjoy it," she replied.

For a while, neither of them said much, but then, Shelby flushed. "This is the first real dress I've made for someone, but I'm glad that I can make you happy," she admitted.

"You do make me happy Shelby. You really do," she replied.

They kissed, and Shelby felt a wave of happiness. When they pulled away, Tasha turned to the side, blushing.

"You know, this is the first time I've really felt this way about someone. I'm so glad to have you here, you know," she said.

"I am too, Tasha. I am too. I'm glad we can overcome this trauma, and learn to recover," Shelby said.

"You're telling me. I feel much more confident now that I've told you the truth. I'm just so glad that you understand, and that you care. It's...nice, really," she replied.

"It is. I'm very happy to be that special someone in your life who you can rely on," Shelby said.

Shelby felt this wave of happiness every time she was around Tasha, and Tasha probably felt the same way. But she didn't want to tell her the truth yet, that she was in love with Tasha. For now, she just wanted to be supportive, to love from afar, and to be the person that would care for her, no matter what the odds may be.

"Anyway, we should probably try to finish everything up. We have the fashion show on Friday, and I'm a little nervous to be back on the catwalk again," Tasha said.

"I understand. But you're not alone this time. You have me, and I'm not going anywhere," Shelby replied.

"Good," Tasha said.

They kissed once more, with Shelby pulling back and blushing. She was just happy Tasha was here with her, and she knew Tasha felt the same way.

They would kill it tomorrow in the fashion show, and they'd make everything perfect no matter what the odds may be, and no matter what came their way.

Chapter Sixteen

Tasha felt her heart race as she looked at Shelby. Every time she was around Shelby, she felt happy, satisfied, and most of all, calm and collected.

There weren't too many women who made her feel like that, none at all really. For the first time, she felt her heart open up. Before Shelby left, Tasha turned to her, giving her a piece of paper.

"Give this to your mom. Tell her she's invited to your show. She wants to see you," Tasha said.

Shelby's eyes opened as she held it there.

"Are you sure?" she said.

"Yes, I want her to see the progress you've made," Tasha said.

Tasha then watched as Shelby started to cry.

"Thank you. This means so much to me Tasha. You don't even understand," she admitted.

"No, I do understand, Shelby. I really do. You want to make things right for you and your mother, and you want to include her in everything that you love. I understand that completely," Tasha said.

"Thank you, Tasha. I'll call her tonight and see if she wants to attend," Shelby said.

"Of course. Hope it goes well," Tasha said.

As they parted ways, Tasha realized the feelings she felt for Shelby were strong. There were a couple times she almost told Shelby she loved her, but she held back. The last thing she wanted was to make Shelby nervous like that.

But, the ache in her heart made her want to say everything to her. After she left the office, she made her way over to the bar once again, sitting down. Nate poured her a drink, and Tasha smiled.

"You always have what I need on tap don't you?" Tasha said with a smirk.

"Of course. I'm trying to make it right for you," he replied.

"Well, the thought is much appreciated. It's nice really," she said.

"I know. Anyway, I was wondering what's up? You seem happier," he said.

She blushed.

"I am happier. I'm very surprised that I am," she said.

"You mean like in general?"

"I really am. By the way Nate, I'm in my first show this weekend. I figured as my loyal bartender whose helped me through nights of drunken stupor, it would only be right if I invited you," Tasha teased.

He laughed. "Sure, if you want me to come to it, I'm free this weekend. I'll be there," he said.

Tasha gave him a ticket, and as she sat there, swishing her drink around, she sighed.

"I think I'm in love," Tasha said.

"You sure? Don't jump into something you feel you're not ready for," he admonished.

"No, I feel ready. I'm not giving up on this," she insisted.

Tasha had been waiting for the right moment. She wanted to tell Shelby that she loved her.

"When do you think you'll tell her then?" Nate asked.

"I think after the show. We're going out. I want to make this special for her," Tasha stated.

"Good. Do that, I'm sure she'll love it," he said.

"I think she will too," Tasha replied.

Tasha felt like she was on top of the world, but she did wonder how things would go tomorrow with Meryl. She wanted to know why Angela invited her too. It bothered her.

The next day, Tasha brought over the dresses, holding them in her hands. Shelby was at the entrance, looking at the guard and speaking.

"I'm telling you, I'm with Tasha," she said.

"No way. Tasha never has assistants," the guard said.

"Excuse me, she's with me," Tasha said.

The guard jumped about ten feet in the air, and for a moment, he just looked at Tasha with a surprised glance.

"Are you serious?" he asked.

"Yes, she's with me. I'm the designer," Tasha said.

"Fair enough. Come on in," the guard muttered.

Tasha smiled, and Shelby walked in right behind her.

"Sorry, that guard is probably just as surprised as most people that I have a partner I work with now," Tasha said.

"You're really that much of a loner?" Shelby asked.

Tasha laughed.

"Well, until you came around, yes," Tasha replied.

Shelby looked at her for a moment with shocked eyes. "I'm sorry. I didn't know that I was that important," she said with a flush.

"Relax. You're very important to me Shelby. I'm glad that I have you," Tasha said.

"I know," she replied.

Tasha motioned toward the end of the hallway. "Head to the room at the very end. That's where they told me that it would be. I need to meet with the directors to find out when we're on," Tasha said.

"All right," Shelby replied.

Tasha walked down the hall. Then, she saw her.

Meryl.

She was standing with Angela, laughing together. Tasha tensed, gripping her fingers and then quickly heading over there. Unfortunately, they were talking to the director too, and it made Tasha tense.

This wasn't going to be pretty.

"Hello," Tasha said.

"Hello, Tasha. How are you? Glad you accepted my invitation to the show," the director said.

"Of course. I was a little surprised some people were allowed," Tasha said, glaring directly at Meryl.

"Well hello to you too Tasha. I'm here with Angela. She said that she needed a new model. I was willing to take the job. Plus, it's been a bit. Aren't you happy to see me again?" she asked.

Tasha cringed at the way she uttered those words.

She was far from happy to see Meryl again, but the last thing she wanted was for her to know that.

"Oh of course. Really *fucking* happy," Tasha said with a sarcastic response.

"I heard you two used to be friends. I figured now might be a perfect time to see each other again," Angela said.

"You know that she's not my friend, Angela. Quit lying," Tasha muttered.

"Excuse me? I know that you two are close. It's what she told me. And she's got a proven track record despite her age," Angela said.

Tasha looked at Meryl. *How many different lies has this bitch told?*

"Well, if you knew the truth, you'd be singing a much different tune," Tasha said.

"Oh really? Well, let's make this interesting. This show in particular has a reward for those who end up generating the crowd's best response. Winner gets to do *whatever* to the loser," Angela said.

Tasha looked at Meryl, who was grinning now.

These two were totally in it together. When Tasha realized this, she felt the anxiety loom in her body, but she knew better than to show fear.

"Fine, you're on," Tasha muttered.

"Ah, a friendly competition. Well, just so you know, both of our models are on at the same time.

So, Meryl, you'll be up with whomever Tasha brought to model. I know you don't tell people who it is beforehand, but I hope the woman you bring forward is ready to rock," the director said.

"Oh, don't worry, she is," Tasha said.

She was ready to put it all on the line, and she would rock it. She'd been waiting for this moment, to go back on the catwalk and win. After she got her information, she left, but she felt Meryl creeping behind her.

"I told you to never speak to me again," Tasha said.

"But Tasha, didn't you miss me?" Meryl asked with a smile.

Tasha looked over at the ruby-haired woman, anger flowing through her body. "I haven't missed you in a long time, Meryl. Leave me alone," she said.

Tasha left, leaving Meryl shocked.

"Fine, if we win, I'll make sure I give you something to remember me by. I'll buy your company, and you'll never be able to design clothing again," Meryl spat.

Tasha turned to her, looking at her with widened eyes. "You... You can't," Tasha said.

"I can, and I will," Meryl replied with a purr.

"I don't believe you."

"Well believe what you want. But this is where we settle it tonight. Either I win and you are out of the business forever. Or, by some goddamn stroke of luck, you win, and I'll acquiesce," she said.

"Fine. You're on," Tasha said.

When she got back to the dressing room, she felt anger flood her body. Shelby walked over, touching her arm.

"She's here, and I need to do well tonight. I have to win or else I'm going to lose everything," Tasha said.

Shelby looked at her, and instead of showing fear like Tasha expected, she saw nothing but happiness in her eyes. Shelby took a deep breath, and after a split second, responded.

"I know Tasha. I'm here for you. I want that as well," she replied.

"I'm glad we're on the same page. Tonight, I'm giving it my all, and I'll stop at nothing to win."

Chapter Seventeen

Shelby could practically taste the conviction off of Tasha's words, but she felt the same way.

"Good, because tonight we'll do it. Together," she replied.

"I'm so glad I have you on my side Shelby. I really am," Tasha replied.

"I am too," Shelby said.

The way they looked at each other was that of pure conviction, and of pure happiness. Shelby then got the dress out, looking at it, and then at you.

"I'll get you ready tonight. You're ready to model these outfits, right?" she asked.

"Well, for this show in particular, there's one highlighter outfit that goes out, and then a few of the sub outfits. I did have a couple of women from my office come here to help with the sub outfits, but the one that we made together, your first dress, is the one that I want to wear tonight. Because, that was one that we made with love, and something that I want…I want to show off to everyone," Tasha said.

Shelby's eyes widened. She didn't know what Tasha wanted to wear, and the fact that Tasha even wanted this surprised her. "You're sure…right?" she asked.

"Of course. I'm very sure," Tasha said.

"Good. I'll do it then. I'm really glad that I get to do this with you," she said.

"I am too Shelby. I really am," Tasha said.

Tasha felt happy about the way things were, and the way that things were going. It made Shelby happy to see the smile on her face.

The models came in, each of them surprised when they saw Tasha there in the corner with the dress on.

"Is she really going to do that?" one of them said.

"Yes. We made these dresses, and we'll make this work," Shelby said.

After a bit, there was another knock. Shelby walked over, expecting it to be one of the women from the other designer's team, but then, it was Danica.

"Danica?" she said.

"Hey, so Tasha asked me to come over and help with the fittings. She also asked me to be a part of the modeling team, so I'm here to get into a dress too," Danica said.

"Seriously?" Shelby gasped.

"Yes. Danica wanted to be a model, but nobody took her seriously. We talked about this a few weeks back, and I offered her a place in my line. I want to show to others that women can be models if they so desire. A person can be themselves. I think it's something bigger than most people expect, and something that the average person isn't expecting here," Tasha said.

Shelby looked over at her friend, the one person who was always here no matter what.

"Well, I'm glad to have you on the team then," Shelby said.

"Great, glad to be here. Let's rock," Danica said.

There would be five models total, counting Danica and Tasha, and Shelby felt like she was the queen of the world. The fact that they were so easy to work with made her happy. She definitely didn't regret any of this.

"Anyway, you ready?" Shelby asked.

"Born ready," Tasha said.

"Yes, everything fits perfectly," Danica said.

"All right, there's about five minutes until the show. Do any last-minute hair and makeup, and we'll go from there," Shelby said.

The models did as they were told, and Shelby felt her heart race. Tasha walked over, taking her hand and holding it.

"You nervous?" Tasha asked.

"Yes. I'm definitely not used to this," Shelby said.

"I'm not either. I'm a little scared myself, but I do think it'll be okay," Tasha said.

Shelby nodded, flushing. "I think it will be too," she replied.

"We'll get through it. And, I'm sure we'll win the bet," Tasha said.

"Yes, we will," Shelby replied.

When it was time, Shelby brought out all of the models, each of them standing there. At first, the other women would go, followed by Danica, and finally, Tasha.

Shelby could feel the anxiety in her body. She didn't want anything to go wrong. When the first women went out, the audience was cheering for them, all of them happy with the way they looked. The other designers brought out a few models too. While they generated some response, it was nothing compared to Tasha and Shelby's designs.

Then, it was Danica's turn. Shelby gave her friend a smile of reassurance before she went out onto the catwalk.

She was nervous, but Shelby noticed how confident she was. She didn't trip thankfully, and as they walked around, Shelby felt happiness as she watched.

Then, it was her turn. Tasha's. Tasha walked forward to where the models were to go out, and when she got to the entrance, Meryl looked over.

"No way," she said.

"Way. I'm here," Tasha said.

"But I thought old ladies couldn't model," Meryl said with a sneer.

"Well, you're here. Why?" Tasha said with a smirk.

Meryl looked at her with surprise. Then, the lights kicked up, the music pumped, and Tasha smiled.

"Go ahead," Tasha said.

"No, you," Meryl replied.

"All right, but it's your funeral," Tasha said.

As she walked forward, Shelby saw the foot. It was extended out, with full intent to trip Tasha. However, Tasha saw it before anything else.

"Nice try," she whispered before digging her stiletto heel into Meryl's foot. She walked out, the crowd in awe at the way she moved about.

Tasha still had it. The way she carried her hips, the way she moved about, the embodiment of sexy as she gyrated her hips, it was a thrill to watch, and Shelby couldn't help but love it. It made her feel excited, made her feel happy, and most of all, made her proud.

Meryl trailed behind her, trying to mask her sore foot, but she did a bad job at it. The intimidation made her shaky, and Tasha watched along with Shelby as she made her way over. When she finally got to Tasha, she grimaced.

"You'll pay for this," she snarled.

"Really now?" Tasha said.

"Yes."

Meryl moved forward, trying to shove Tasha off. Then, Tasha smiled, moving out of the way for a split second. It caused Meryl to cry out, and soon, she fell to the ground. All of the people immediately gasped as Meryl lay there, knocked out for a split second.

"I don't know why she did that. I guess she was a little klutzy," Tasha said.

The crowd laughed, and Tasha walked back. When Tasha finally got off the stage, she turned to Shelby, smiling.

"Thank you so much for warning me about her," Tasha said.

"I tried my best, but you seemed to know," Shelby replied.

"She's always pulling dirty tricks. This is definitely not a surprise," Tasha said.

"All right, and that concludes our show. Let's bring out all of our designers and models to give out the grand prize! It's the award for best in show, based on audience response and input," the director said.

They all walked out, with Tasha smiling and beaming. Angela was grimacing and trying to nurse the shaken Meryl.

"All right everyone. Time to discuss everyone that we saw tonight. There was an impressive turnout, and a couple of mishaps, but I do have to say that there was one clear designer that showed strength that was unparalleled. And that of course was Tasha!" the director said.

Tasha motioned for Shelby to come forward. As she did, the crowd screamed. Tasha stood there, beaming, and Shelby felt like it was a dream.

"Thank you everyone. This is the first time I've modeled in five years. I was the subject of an abusive relationship here in the modeling community. Meryl here and I have some unsavory history, and I decided to get back into it. I've been known as the 'one woman army' for a long time, but the truth is, I couldn't have done it with my partner here. This is Shelby everyone. She's someone that I managed to convince to work with me. Whether it was desperation or something more, I don't regret everything I've done with her. So thank you Shelby. And I'm happy to bring my creativity to all of you," Tasha said.

The crowd cheered, and Shelby had tears in her eyes. Her mother was in the audience, giving a standing ovation to them. But then, Tasha reached forward, giving Shelby a kiss for a brief second.

"And I want to come forward. Shelby is now my partner, both a work partner and a romantic partner. I care about her, and I really do appreciate all that she's done. Thanks Shelby. I do like that you're here with me," Tasha said.

"Shelby wanted to cry. She felt happy, secure, and most of all, ready to have a better life.

"Thank you, Tasha. I'm ready too," Shelby said.

She embraced Tasha, and the crowd cheered. This was the happiest moment of her life, and she knew that she was so happy she felt like she was in a whole new world. This was her life now, and she had someone who cared about her more than anything else.

And boy did that feel good.

Chapter Eighteen

Tasha felt happy, for the first time in a long while. But she couldn't predict what would happen next.

After they finished, Meryl came over, glaring at Tasha. "You won this time, but don't think I'm just going to let you get away with this," she said.

"Meryl, it's over. I don't want to see you again. I've already informed the directors and other designers about your past. They don't want to work with you. Angela will also be associated with you if she decides to stay here too. You won't win," Tasha said.

She looked at Tasha, and then sighed. "I thought you loved me," Meryl muttered.

"In the past, yes. Now? No. I don't love you at all Meryl, I wish you would just leave," Tasha said.

Tasha glared at Meryl, and Meryl tensed.

"Fine. You win," she muttered.

She quickly ran off, leaving Tasha alone.

"Are you okay?" Shelby asked.

"I've been better. I'm just a little surprised really. I didn't expect to do what I did out there, but it changed my life. Thank you, Shelby. I do owe you," Tasha said.

If it weren't for Shelby, Tasha would probably never have gotten on stage. She really did love Shelby, in her own way.

"I'm glad you're happy Tasha. I'm glad that I can do so much for you," Shelby said.

Tasha blushed.

"By the way, I wouldn't mind if you went with me to dinner next Monday. You can always take off from work and we can go together," Tasha said.

She wondered what Shelby might say. She could have refused, but Shelby nodded instead, her eyes bright with excitement.

"I'd love to go out. Just the two of us," she said.

Tasha beamed. She felt like she finally got to do what she wanted to do. She hadn't had a date in a long time. Not since she went out on a pity date so long ago.

When Monday rolled around, Tasha waited for Shelby, dressed in a red dress that was slinky, and hugged her curves. Shelby arrived, dressed in a black gown that had a low-cut, plunging neckline, and also had a tight frame to it. Tasha looked at her, her eyes wide with surprise.

"Wow, you look amazing," she said.

"Thank you," Shelby said.

Tasha's eyes continued to look at her body, her mind racing with surprise and awe. She loved this, and she knew that Shelby felt the same way.

"Well, ready to go? I thought of the perfect place to go to," she said.

"Oh really? Where to?" Shelby inquired.

"You'll see," Tasha said with a wink.

It was a place she always wanted to go, the gardens restaurant. It was situated in an observatory, and Tasha scored some amazing connections to actually get in. Tonight would be the night, and when she parked, Shelby's eyes widened.

"I've always wanted to try this place," she said.

"Good. That makes two of us. I promised myself I would never come here until I had a partner, and well, this is it," she said.

Shelby blushed. "I'm glad that we can have this together," she said.

"I'm glad too," Tasha replied.

They walked in, and the server showed them to a big table that overlooked all of the gardens.

"This is the best seat in the house!" Shelby said.

"I wanted to treat you right. Tonight, it's about us. It's not about the gowns we made, or the fashion show. Tonight, I just want to make you happy. I haven't had a chance to do that yet. I'm really glad that you're here with me Shelby," Tasha said.

She meant what she said. Shelby blushed in response.

"I know that you do. I know you care a lot about me. It's very nice really," Shelby said.

"You make me happy, Shelby. It's something very few people can achieve, at least for me. It's weird being with someone who cares so much, and someone who actually does give a damn. I really do appreciate all of this," Tasha admitted.

She didn't want this feeling to go away. She wanted to experience it forever.

The server came, and Tasha ordered a big bottle of wine. Shelby's eyes widened as it came over, the red liquid filling the glasses.

They drank wine and looked into each other's eyes, the passion, desire, and need were growing.

"I'm glad I can take you out, Shelby. I loved what we did at the show the other night," Tasha said.

"I did too. I'm going to be honest Tasha. This is the first time I've truly had a date with another woman," Shelby said with a blush.

Tasha's eyes widened in surprise. Shelby was about twelve years younger than she was. Shelby didn't have as much experience, but she hadn't gone on a date or anything?

"Are you serious?" Tasha asked.

"Yes. I've never had the opportunity to experience that romance that I've wanted to feel for a long time. But here I am with you, and I'm so damn happy about that," she said.

Tasha smiled, looking at Shelby with a grin of excitement.

"I'm glad that you're in my life, Shelby," Tasha said.

"I am too. It's weird, I expected that one day I'd get to experience this with someone, but I never imagined you would make me feel like a princess," she said.

"I'm glad that you're happy," Tasha said.

"I really am, Tasha. You've changed my life. You showed my mom that I can make a career out of designing, and I can really be myself. You make me happy knowing this is real, and that I can be happy," Shelby replied.

"I'm glad Shelby. You're a big part of my life, and I'm glad that I can make you feel good on a day like today. For me, it's kind of the same. Sure, I've had dates in the past, but they weren't the same. It feels like a whole new life has come forth, and we can share it together," Tasha stated.

Shelby's eyes widened, and as she leaned in and grabbed Tasha's hand, she felt a radiant warmth from this.

"By the way, how did the public react to us?" Shelby asked.

"Oh, they're happy about it. A lot of people just wanted to see me happy," Tasha admitted.

She didn't feel happy in the past, and this was all novel to her, but for Tasha, she loved everything about this, and she knew that Shelby was happy as well.

"So, nobody is upset?" Shelby said.

"Well, people are mad at Meryl for what she did. I don't blame them. I was pretty pissed at her. But I'm glad that she's getting what she deserves," Tasha said.

"What she did wasn't cool," Shelby stated.

"I agree. I'm just surprised she had the audacity to come back after all this time. I guess she couldn't manipulate anyone else anymore, and now she needed to move onto something else," Tasha said.

"Also, I've talked with my mom about my dad. So far, they're trying to work things out between them. It isn't going swimmingly, but they're trying," she said.

"I figured. I know how it can be. I mean, it seems like she does love her partner, but there are some things that need to be worked out," Tasha said.

"Like I know that they do, but the whole mess with me being an oops baby has taken a toll on their life. They stuck together because of me, which I understand, but I wish they were honest with each other, and admitted that there were problems," Shelby said.

"I know. But that's not your relationship. I'm sure that your mother has her reasons for doing what she did, but you've got to understand that, if you let that get to you, you'll feel worse," Tasha said.

"You're right, you're right. I don't know, I think about it a lot," Shelby replied.

"I understand. But, let's just spend our time together. Forget about the feelings that others make you feel. Let's be happy together," Tasha said.

Tasha meant every word. When Shelby looked at her with those wide eyes, she felt her heart lurch in response. Tasha did love Shelby, and she loved her a whole lot. she felt like she really did have those feelings on hand, and they weren't just little things which were eating away at her.

"Thank you, Tasha. I do love you, you know," Shelby said.

Tasha blushed. "I do too Shelby. You make me feel very happy," she replied.

"I feel the same way. I'm so glad you took a chance on me that day, you know, with the dress thing," Shelby said with a flush.

"I'm glad too Shelby. I'm delighted that we can be like this," Tasha said.

The excitement in her eyes made Tasha feel like all of this was indeed worth it. Dinner was simple, and as they looked downward, they saw the couples that were there.

"I love that I can actually have this moment with you. It's so romantic and so wonderful for me," Shelby said.

Tasha smiled, and she felt a whole feeling of happiness hit her body.

"Well, I will say that no matter what happens next, we do have each other," Tasha said with a smile, extending her hand and holding it. Shelby beamed.

It was the perfect moment, and for Tasha, she wanted nothing more than to experience this moment. It was like a riveting breath of fresh air. For Tasha, she felt like all of the worries that she had in life, all of the sorrow, the pain, and the struggles that she felt up to this point were now gone.

Tasha felt like everything that was holding her back in the past was just that, the past. Right now, she felt like her heart was open, and the future was looking bright.

After they finished dinner, they walked around, each of them as they looked at the observatory.

"Do you want to go over to the top of the tower?" Tasha asked.

There was a tower in the middle that people could go up. Currently, there was no line, and Shelby nodded.

"Yes, I'd love that," Shelby replied.

"Good. Let's go."

They waited in line, heading to the very top. Most people didn't pay mind to either of them, which made Tasha happy and relaxed. She was glad that nobody seemed to care all that much about everything that was happening, and the interactions at hand.

They grasped each other's hands, looking at the world below. All the people in cars, the hustle and bustle of the city, it all felt so detached from the world they were in right now, the one they were in together.

"Hey Tasha, there's something I'd like to say," Shelby admitted.

"What is it?" Tasha asked.

Shelby flushed, but then, she leaned in, grasping her hand, holding it there and smiling.

"I love you more than I ever expected to love someone. This is the best moment of my life, and I'm glad that I get to experience it with you," Shelby replied.

Tasha smiled, leaning in and grasping her hand, a warm smile on her face. She felt the redness on her face spread all the way over to her body.

"I love you too Shelby. My heart feels whole. I don't feel worried about future. I'm elated with the way we've managed to make this work, and the future we've built for ourselves," Tasha replied.

Shelby's' smile radiated through the air. Soon, they were kissing. It was a small, succulent kiss. As they continued to let their lips and tongue move, Shelby seemed to push her tongue in further, letting her mouth open so Tasha could take control, pushing her tongue in once again. The two of them stayed like that, enjoying the feeling of each other, that is until Tasha pulled away. She flushed as she looked about, and then at Shelby.

"Why don't we take this back to the apartment," she said.

"Sure, I'd love that," Shelby replied.

Tasha took her hand, heading down the stairs and over to the car. She didn't mind kissing Shelby in public, but she could tell a few people were a little shocked at the upfront nature of it, and Tasha didn't want anyone looking at them like that. When they finally made their way over and into the car, Shelby gave her a hot, passionate kiss in the car, pulling away and blushing.

"I'm just so glad to have you," she said.

"I am too Shelby, but we should probably not be so open with the PDA and all, since we're both kind of known," Tasha admonished.

"Right. Sorry about that," she said.

Tasha smiled.

"All good. I just didn't want to make things awkward for us or anything," she admitted.

Shelby nodded, and soon, they quickly made their way home. It was the perfect moment when they got inside and they quickly moved to the bedroom. As Tasha watched Shelby touching her hair, and looking into her beautiful green eyes, her heart ached.

"You look wonderful," she purred.

"I could say the same thing about you," Shelby replied with a smile.

They felt their desires grow stronger, the aching need making them both want something more. They kissed. As they did so, they felt their need for each other grow, and the love they shared taking them to new heights.

Chapter Nineteen

Shelby quickly kissed Tasha back, and as the two of them embraced in the confines of her home, Shelby felt happy, and she felt her body ache for more from her. Shelby knew that Tasha enjoyed this just as much as she did, and the emotion they shared was something that only they knew.

Shelby felt it was the perfect moment. She waited for this forever, wanted this romantic interaction, and she didn't care what happened next. She just wanted to stay with Tasha forever. The feeling of their bodies touching each other, the excitement that grew within, all of this culminated into feelings that touched her on new, more amazing levels, and made her ache for everything more.

Tasha then moved her, pushing her against the wall and holding her hands up. Shelby gasped as the two of them let their lips touch, and their bodies move. It was the most perfect moment. She wanted to just stay like that forever.

She wondered if she could just freeze time. It would be silly, but it was how she felt. Tasha then pulled away, a dribble of spit connecting their lips. They both breathed heavily, but not before Tasha spoke.

"I love you Shelby. Tonight, I want to make us both feel good. I got a few toys for this moment, and I can't wait to use them on you," she purred.

"I can't wait either," Shelby said.

They let their lips touch and their bodies move closer, the feeling of happiness and desire washing over them. Shelby felt like she was in heaven, and as Tasha took control, pulling her away and guiding her toward the bedroom, she felt like she was at the mercy of this beautiful woman, and she wouldn't have it any other way.

When Tasha and she got to the bedroom, Tasha pushed her on the bed, causing her to gasp in surprise. Tasha got on top of her, letting her lips move toward her own, kissing her with a full, wrought-iron passion that Shelby couldn't get enough of. The two of them stayed like that for what felt like forever, then Tasha started to move downward, letting her lips lightly cascade and touch Shelby's body.

Shelby let out a small purr, excitement growing within. Then Tasha started to bite down on the skin, nibbling on the flesh and making Shelby moan aloud with full-fledged desire.

"Are you doing all right?" Tasha said.

"Oh God yes. Mark me. Make me yours," Shelby said.

Tasha let out a purr, and soon, she did that, digging her lips deep into Shelby's skin, causing Shelby to let out a small moan of complete, utter pleasure, and she wanted to just remember this moment for the rest of her life. She didn't want to forget it, and she knew that Tasha was the same way.

As she bit down and nibbled on the skin, Shelby let out a series of gasps, moans, and mewls, embracing the full pleasure of the moment as Tasha then started to push her lips toward the apex of her chest, kissing and sucking on the sweet flesh there. Her hands moved toward Shelby's dress, touching the back of it and looking at her.

"You look so gorgeous in it. It's a shame I have to take it off," she said.

"You'll love what's underneath too," Shelby replied with a smile.

Tasha moaned, then pulled the garment off Shelby's body, sliding the dress down and tossing it to the side. Shelby gasped as she felt Tasha tear it off her body, exposing her skin to the air around. Tasha looked at her body, her eyes widening at how gorgeous Shelby's' body was.

Shelby bought this bra and panties set the other day, and when Tasha's eyes widened at the sight of the black garment covering her body, it made Shelby flush.

Tasha moved her lips toward the top of her breasts, which were spilling out of the cups. Shelby gasped as Tasha's hands cupped them, kissing them softly before moving her hand to the back of the garment, pulling it off her body and tossing it to the floor.

Shelby gasped as she felt her breasts exposed, her cold nipples immediately hardening in response. Shelby watched as Tasha took them in her mouth sucking and teasing on the soft nipples, making Shelby let out sounds that she didn't even know existed.

She loved every passing moment of this, the excitement of the moment, and the feelings that this made her feel.

She craved more from Tasha, the passion, the desire, the excitement only making her crave this feeling again and again. Tasha seemed to be enjoying this too, letting her tongue snake out and swish over the top of it, sucking on the very top before Tasha moved toward the other nipple, pinching and letting it rest on her hands.

Shelby felt the excitement grow, and the feelings of the moment driving her mad.

It was making her crave everything that she desired, the aching feeling of it all making her go crazy.

Tasha noticed that desperation, and Shelby was glad to see her move her hands toward her waist, holding it there and letting her hands dance against the straps of the garment.

"This is so cute, but I want to continue to make you feel good," Tasha said.

"Please," Shelby said, her body warm with desperation.

She wanted to feel the pleasure of her lover, and it was obvious that Tasha was feeling the same way, judging by the little cheeky grin she had on her face.

Tasha's hands moved toward her waist, touching her body slightly and making her gasp in surprise. Tasha then moved her hands downwards, kissing Shelby's thighs and touching them slightly. She moved back, taking off her dress as well, and Shelby's' hands moved toward the back of her bra, undoing the clasp, pulling it off. Tasha gazed as Shelby looked at her with anticipation.

"You look wonderful," she purred.

"Thank you," Tasha said with a smile.

Shelby's hands moved toward her nipples, touching them slightly. Tasha was soon in her lap, grinding against Shelby, the pleasure of the moment making her shiver with delight. The two of them moaned as they touched. It was the perfect moment for Shelby. She started to push her body against Tasha's own, kissing as she did.

For Shelby, she felt it was the perfect moment, and she just wanted to spend this time with Tasha. But then, Tasha moved, kissing up her thighs, and for a moment, she looked over at Shelby with anticipation in her eyes. She moved her hands toward the sides of her panties, undoing them and pulling them downwards. Tasha dove right in, kissing and teasing every single part of her.

The way Tasha touched her was enough to drive her mad, and as Tasha did this, Shelby started to gasp, touching the sheets and gripping them with delight. She then started to look at Tasha with delight, crying out loud at the sensations that Tasha provided to her.

The way she kissed, touched, and pushed her lips deep into her, pushing her tongue out and moving inside, made Shelby start to cry out in pleasure, the excitement of the moment driving her to the point of madness.

Shelby loved everything about this, and as she felt Tasha push her tongue upwards, hitting that one part of her, that sweet spot, she then started to cry out, feeling the sudden force of her orgasm loom over her body.

She didn't want to cum yet. She was enjoying this far too much, but she also knew that she was super close. When Tasha pushed her tongue up, grazing that spot once again, pushing it upwards, Shelby then started to cry out, feeling the sudden excitement of the moment. Then, came hard. She loved everything about it, enjoying the moment, then relaxed.

It was one of the best orgasms she's had in a long time. When she looked at Tasha, she kissed her, and the two of them made out for a bit. But then, Shelby got an idea.

"What are you doing?" Tasha said.

"Returning the favor," Shelby told her with a purr.

She then spread Tasha's legs apart, pushing her tongue inside, teasing the same way that Tasha did to her. Tasha then tensed up, holding her head there and crying out.

Shelby wasn't a pro at this by any means, and she felt like her actions were messy to say the least, but she seemed to be doing decently, as she pushed her tongue deep into her. She then moved her hands toward her clit, thumb resting on there and teasing it.

"Ahh fuck!" Tasha said, and then, she immediately tensed up in surprise, but not before relaxing in the process.

After she came, she moved backwards, and as they looked at each other, they smiled.

"I want to try something else," Tasha said.

"Sure," Shelby replied.

Tasha fumbled for something in her drawer, and when she pulled it out, Shelby's eyes widened. It was one of those double-ended dildos that she saw around. She never thought that Tasha would get something like this, but as she started to look at Tasha, she had a feeling that she was in for an amazing moment, and she was definitely excited about this.

Tasha smiled, moving one side into herself. She let out a small gasp as it filled her up, and Shelby couldn't help but watch with both awe and amazement. She loved that Tasha was enjoying this, and then, once Tasha finished pushing it in, she looked at Shelby with a grin.

"Ready?" she asked.

"Sure," Shelby said, blushing at the idea of this. She looked at Tasha, and then, for a brief second, she watched as Tasha then pushed the dildo into her.

"Ahh!" Shelby cried out, feeling it fill her up. She wanted to wince in both pain, but also in pleasure, and when she looked at Tasha, she could see the delightful grin on her face. She wanted to take this because she was excited to see what this would feel like.

After a few second, the entire dildo was inside her. Shelby was nervous, but she was also happy to experience the moment with Tasha. It was the perfect moment, and she definitely enjoyed everything about this as well. For a second, Tasha didn't move, and she looked at Tasha with surprise in her eyes, but then, she started to move against there and when she did, Shelby cried out in both pain, but also in utter pleasure.

It was different, but after the initial shock, she loved it, pushing her body against it, crying out in pleasure Tasha was soon on top of her, her smaller frame also riding the other side. She grasped Shelby's' breasts touching and teasing them there, looking over at Shelby with a smile of excitement on her face. She loved everything about this and didn't want the moment to ever go away.

After a second, the two started to kiss, making out as Tasha started to push the dildo into her, moaning in response. Shelby grasped Tasha's body, holding it there as they continued to ride each side, and as they did this, it was the perfect moment. For a long time, they just continued to do this, when suddenly, Tasha pushed her fingertips toward her clit, touching it there. that alone sent Shelby into a tizzy, crying out in pleasure as she started to tense up, holding her there as she cried out.

Shortly after, Tasha then did the same thing, holding her there as she cried out against her body. For a long time, neither of them moved. It was the perfect moment, and neither of them wanted to spoil it. Tasha didn't know what to say, and neither did Shelby.

"Are you all right?" Tasha asked.

"Wonderful really," Shelby said.

It was one of the best orgasms of her life, and as she touched Tasha's face, she saw the smile on her face.

"Happy Valentine's Day," she said.

"Happy Valentine's Day to you too," Shelby replied with a smile.

They kissed, and continued to make love throughout the night, and as Shelby continued to kiss, touch, and feel Tasha against her, she never wanted to forget this feeling.

The feeling of making love, the feeling of experiencing love, and all of that. It was perfect, and Shelby couldn't help but love every moment of it, and she definitely was happy with the life that she had, and the future she created for herself.

Chapter Twenty

About a year had passed, and for Tasha, life couldn't be any better.

Ever since that night, that Valentine's Day that they confessed their love, things had changed for them. Sure, Shelby graduated shortly after that night, and she did stick around with Tasha, but instead of being a mere intern, they were known as partners in crime.

"Are you sure you're down with being partners? I mean, I'm fine with it, but it's your business. You're known for always working alone," Shelby pointed out.

"I want to do this. I wouldn't ask you otherwise," Tasha insisted.

"Good, I'm glad. I didn't know if you really meant it or not. I've really liked having you around, and I really like being with you Tasha. I just didn't want to pressure you or anything," Shelby replied.

"Nah, you're wonderful Shelby. I'm really glad to have you around," Tasha insisted.

She meant it, and as Shelby looked at her, giving her a kiss on the lips and feeling the excitement of the moment, the two of them insisted that they would be there for each other, no matter what the world may bring forth, and no matter what happened next.

Business changed. Tasha was getting more and more orders for dresses than she expected. Being a designer was her passion, and she was always moderately successful, but after this, everything changed for the better. She wasn't feeling pressured by the worries of the past, and she instead, looked forward to the future.

Shelby also seemed happy too. Shelby always seemed to talk to her about everything, and she would always run ideas by Tasha, no matter how silly they were. Tasha appreciated Shelby, since she was more important than anyone else in the world, at least according to her.

They had the feelings of love and adoration for each other. It was only making Tasha want to spend the rest of her life with her even more.

About a year later, Shelby came in, her eyes happy and a smile on her face.

"Guess what," she said.

"What's up?" Tasha said.

"My mom and dad aren't divorcing. They talked, and it seems that they were able to really work this out. I'm surprised, but also...very happy with this," she said.

Tasha grinned, feeling good about this.

"I'm so glad Shelby," Tasha said, holding Shelby there and kissing her. She was happy for her girlfriend, and it made Tasha appreciate her even more. Given how supportive Shelby was toward her, it only made sense that this would make Tasha happy as well.

Life continued to be good for them. Business was booming, and they were booked for more shows. But Tasha wanted nothing more than to just spend time with Shelby and experience the thrill of the moment together. But Tasha wanted something more.

After a bit, she realized what it was. She wanted to marry Shelby.

Sure, she was older, and usually marriage was saved for younger people, but Tasha didn't think that it would be a bad thing. But, where would she ask her?

Tasha was both excited for this, but she also feared asking her. She didn't want to come off too strong. But, one night at the bar, Tasha sat down with Nate, her best friend, and he spoke.

"You should just tell her in the most memorable place for both of you. Or maybe, a new, memorable location. You could go to dinner or something," he said.

"I don't think so. I want it to be really memorable…wait a moment, I've got it. You're cool with me sending ring pictures, right?" Tasha said.

"Of course! I'm just happy for you. I've been seeing you less at the bar since you got with her, and while I've missed the stories and the tabs, I also know that you need this Tasha. You've been sad for far too long, and that whole mess with your ex messed you up for a while," he pointed out.

She nodded. "You're telling me," Tasha said.

"Besides, I feel it's only right," he said.

"You're right. I deserve to be happy, and I do want to marry her. It doesn't have to be right away, but I want to…I want to express my love you know?" she said.

After that, Tasha changed. She felt inspired to make Shelby the happiest person alive, and she would do this no matter what. After she finished that drink, she went out, looking around for the perfect ring. She finally found one at a jeweler a few days later, getting it.

Now that she had it, all that was left was to give it to her.

"I'm nervous, but I know I'll make her happy," Tasha said to herself.

After work that day, Tasha went over to Shelby's office, knocking on the door. Shelby started to open the door, looking at her for a brief moment before speaking.

"Hello," Tasha said.

"Hello, Tasha. Is everything all right?" Shelby asked.

"Yes. There's just something I'd like to talk to you about. Can we go to the roof?" Tasha asked.

She figured this would be the perfect place. They went up there from time to time to chat, but never like this. Shelby agreed, and soon after they got up there, Shelby looked at her with surprise on her face.

"What's the matter? You look like you have something important to talk to me about?" she asked.

"I do. Shelby, I've been grappling with how to approach you about it," Tasha said.

"What do you mean? What are you grappling with?" Shelby inquired.

Tasha blushed, but then, she looked at Shelby, flushing.

"Shelby, I really do appreciate all you've done for me, and everything that's happened between us has changed me for the better. I want to be a better person to you, Shelby. I want to give you this," Tasha said.

"Give me what?" Shelby asked.

She didn't seem to get it, but then, Tasha started to move her body, getting down on one knee. Shelby's eyes widened, and she gasped.

"No way," she said.

"Yes Shelby. I've been meaning to ask for a long time cause you matter so much to me, but I don't want to make it awkward for either of us. So, I'll ask now. Will you marry me?" Tasha asked.

She felt her heart race as Shelby just stood there, looking at her with surprise on her face.

"I want to Tasha. Are you sure? You want this too, right?"

"More than anything else Shelby," Tasha said.

"Then, yes, I'll marry you," Shelby replied

Tasha pulled her into her arms, holding her there. For a long time, neither of them left, nor did they want to. It was something that made Shelby happy, and Tasha could see it in her eyes. She started to cry, and Tasha held her there, caressing her back.

"I'm so happy. Thank you, Shelby," Tasha said.

"I am too Tasha. I love you so goddamn much. No matter what happens next, come hell or high water, I'll be here for you Tasha," Shelby said.

"And I will as well. You've changed me for the better Shelby, and for that, I thank you," Tasha replied.

They shared a tender kiss, knowing true happiness was found within themselves, and the solace they felt as well.